"Haven't you ever felt like doing anything crazy?" Maxim asked as he brushed the side of Annegret's face with the back of his hand.

A shiver of response took her. She tried for flippancy. "If I do, I lie down until the impulse passes."

"And if it doesn't?"

He stepped into the room and pulled the door shut behind him. She heard a click as he engaged the lock. The eager leap of her heart contradicted her logical mind warning her that she didn't want this—didn't want to acknowledge what was between them.

She'd told herself as long as they ignored it, it would go away. It wasn't fair of Maxim to change the rules now. Why didn't he simply take her out to dinner? They could discuss her ideas for his film, keep things on an even keel between them.

Pretend nothing else was happening here.

But then he took her in his arms and it was impossible to pretend any longer.

Dear Reader,

Discover a guilt-free way to enjoy this holiday season. Treat yourself to four calorie-free, but oh-so-satisfying brand-new Silhouette Romance titles this month.

Start with *Santa Brought a Son* (#1698) by Melissa McClone. This heartwarming reunion romance is the fourth book in Silhouette Romance's new six-book continuity, MARRYING THE BOSS'S DAUGHTER.

Would a duty-bound prince forsake tradition to marry an enchanting commoner? Find out in *The Prince & the Marriage Pact* (#1699), the latest episode in THE CARRAMER TRUST miniseries by reader favorite Valerie Parv.

Then, it's anyone's guess if a wacky survival challenge can end happily ever after. Join the fun as the romantic winners of a crazy contest are revealed in *The Bachelor's Dare* (#1700) by Shirley Jump.

And in Donna Clayton's *The Nanny's Plan* (#1701), a would-be sophisticate is put through the ringer by a drop-dead gorgeous, absentminded professor and his rascally twin nephews.

So pick a cozy spot, relax and enjoy all four of these tender holiday confections that Silhouette Romance has cooked up just for you.

Happy holidays!

Mavis C. Allen
Associate Senior Editor

Please address questions and book requests to:
Silhouette Reader Service
U.S.: 3010 Walden Ave., P.O. Box 1325, Buffalo, NY 14269
Canadian: P.O. Box 609, Fort Erie, Ont. L2A 5X3

The Prince & the Marriage Pact

VALERIE PARV

SILHOUETTE *Romance* ®

Published by Silhouette Books

America's Publisher of Contemporary Romance

To the "first" Annegret, with much affection.

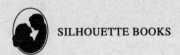 SILHOUETTE BOOKS

ISBN 0-373-19699-7

THE PRINCE & THE MARRIAGE PACT

Copyright © 2003 by Valerie Parv

This edition published by arrangement with Harlequin Books S.A.

® and TM are trademarks of Harlequin Books S.A., used under license. Trademarks indicated with ® are registered in the United States Patent and Trademark Office, the Canadian Trade Marks Office and in other countries.

Visit Silhouette at www.eHarlequin.com

Printed in U.S.A.

Books by Valerie Parv

Silhouette Romance

The Leopard Tree #507
The Billionaire's Baby Chase #1270
Baby Wishes and Bachelor Kisses #1313
*The Monarch's Son #1459
*The Prince's Bride-To-Be #1465
*The Princess's Proposal #1471
Booties and the Beast #1501
Code Name: Prince #1516
†Crowns and a Cradle #1621
†The Baron & the Bodyguard #1627
†The Marquis and the Mother-to-Be #1633
††The Viscount & the Virgin #1691
††The Princess & the Masked Man #1695
††The Prince & the Marriage Pact #1699

Silhouette Intimate Moments

Interrupted Lullaby #1095
Royal Spy #1154

*The Carramer Crown
†The Carramer Legacy
††The Carramer Trust

VALERIE PARV

With twenty million copies of her books sold, including three Waldenbooks' bestsellers, it's no wonder Valerie Parv is known as Australia's queen of romance, and is the recognized media spokesperson for all things romantic. Valerie is married to her own romantic hero, Paul, a former crocodile hunter in Australia's tropical north.

These days he's a cartoonist and the two live in the country's capital city of Canberra, where both are volunteer zoo guides, sharing their love of animals with visitors from all over the world. Valerie continues to write her page-turning novels because they affirm her belief in love and happy endings. As she says, "Love gives you wings, romance helps you fly." Keep up with Valerie's latest releases at www.silromanceauthors.com.

From Sea to Stars

Oh Carramer, our Carramer,
It is of you we proudly sing,
Once scattered isles,
None now divide,
From sea to stars, our freedom rings.

To you we pledge, oh Carramer,
Our hearts and hands, our everything,
To grow in peace
And harmony,
From sea to stars, as freedom rings.

The cherished kingdom, Carramer,
No matter what the future brings,
Through love and courage
Shows the way
From sea to stars, as freedom rings.

Chapter One

Annegret West felt a rush of anticipation as she ventured deeper into the corridors of Merrisand Castle. The sounds of the wedding reception gradually faded behind her as she told herself there was no harm in looking around. If these areas had been off-limits to visitors, surely there would have been security guards to direct her back to the reception rooms?

Considering that the groom was a key member of the Royal Protection Detail, and many of his colleagues were occupied attending the wedding, she wasn't surprised when no one questioned her right to be here.

Her air of confidence was the key, she knew. She was well dressed, as befitted a guest at a wedding taking place in a royal castle, and she walked with the assurance of someone who knew exactly where she was going.

Passing a gold-framed mirror, she caught a glimpse of a statuesque blonde with short-cropped hair feathered around her ears. Her slender frame was skimmed by a sleeveless, navy linen dress, although she wouldn't have minded if her tiny, cream lace cardigan had buttoned over breasts a size or two larger. She smiled at her reflection, recalling a famous duchess saying one could never be too thin or too rich. Annegret's genes had taken care of the thin part. She was still working on the rest.

As producer of the television show, *Behind Closed Doors,* she had learned to trust her instincts. Right now they were leading her deeper into the castle. She was interested in the unique situation of the prince who ruled the castle, and intended to research his story for a possible program.

The show was on its summer break, allowing her to come to Carramer for the wedding of her former school friend, Donna, to the handsome security man, Kevin Jordan. With the ceremony and speeches over for the moment, and the wedding breakfast well under way, Annegret felt free to wander until she found what she was looking for.

And there it was.

She slowed as she approached a huge oil painting in an ornate gold frame. She had seen enough reproductions to recognize it on sight. Painted a hundred seventy-five years ago by a renowned Carramer artist, the *Champagne Pact* depicted the ancestor of the present prince sealing a bargain with a rich merchant by the name of Soral. A bargain with the devil, as history recorded it.

The painting gained its name from the goblets of champagne the figures were raising to seal their agreement. The merchant had provided a vast sum of money to finance development in the province of

Taures, where Merrisand Castle was located. In return, Soral had extracted the prince's vow that for the next two centuries, if a firstborn son of Taures married a woman not of royal blood, the crown would pass to the Soral family.

Fiendishly clever, Annegret thought. According to history, the merchant had known that the prince was madly in love with a commoner, and had assumed the crown was within his grasp. But the prince had outwitted the merchant by sacrificing his love for the good of the crown. Annegret gathered that princes of Taures had been doing much the same thing ever since.

She had long been fascinated by the Champagne Pact itself, as well as the famous painting. Knowing that at least one branch of royalty was doomed to be unlucky in love gave her enormous satisfaction.

Recognizing her own bias in this particular area, Annegret felt a twinge of conscience. While working in the Australian diplomatic service, her mother had fallen in love with an equerry to Prince Frederick of Ehrenberg, then his country's ambassador to Australia. After promising to marry her mother and take her home to his country, the equerry had instead left Debra West alone and pregnant with his child.

Annegret lifted her shoulders in a shrug. So she wasn't a fan of royalty. It was hardly surprising, given that she was the child the man had turned his back on. The only correspondence her mother had received from the man was a letter soon after Annegret was born, telling her that she wouldn't be hearing from him again.

Ehrenberg's borders had been closed to foreigners for most of Annegret's life, so she and her mother couldn't seek out the man to demand an explanation. Not that Annegret wanted to. She told herself that he had done her mother a favor, leaving his child to be raised in Australia. Had he taken her mother home to Ehrenberg with him, Annegret would be there still, confined within the mountain kingdom, cut off from the rest of the world. If it wasn't for the unhappiness her father had caused her mother, Annegret would have no regrets at all.

Dismissing the thought, she studied the painting. If she hadn't known it was so old, she would have been confused by the strong resemblance of that prince to the present-day prince of Taures, Maxim de Marigny. He had put in an appearance at the wedding to wish the couple well.

He was amazingly good-looking, a fact that hadn't escaped her notice at the ceremony. As dark in coloring as his ancestor in the painting, Prince Maxim had the most amazing cobalt-blue eyes. As the guests left the chapel, the prince's gaze had fixed on her for a few seconds, sending a shiver of response down her spine. Although tempted, she hadn't looked away, and had caught a glimmer of amusement in his expression, as if he had expected her to lower her lashes, and was pleased when she met his gaze unflinchingly.

Pure fantasy, she told herself. The product of working too hard to wrap up her most recent series before leaving Australia. Still, she couldn't deny that he had noticed her. She had certainly noticed him.

He possessed a worldly look she found herself wondering about. He hadn't appeared overly pampered, yet his job as administrator of the Merrisand charitable trust had to be a sinecure. With a thousand years of royal tradition behind him, he obviously didn't need to work for a living.

He hadn't looked as inbred as she'd expected, either. His wide, strong mouth was far from effete, and his athletic build suggested he took as much care of himself as Annegret herself did. She liked that, having little patience with people who took no pride in their appearance. She didn't care whether they were tall or short, heavy or slender, as long as they made the best of what they had.

There was no denying that Prince Maxim did so, she thought. What he had amounted to a devastatingly masculine package. Her mental assessment had included long limbs and a lithe body encased in a dark suit that was a monument to tailoring excellence.

But there was something more—a commanding quality that owed nothing to breeding or tailoring. Had he been the lowliest commoner, Maxim would still have been an impressive man, she conceded. He couldn't have helped it.

Annoyed with her train of thought, she turned away from the painting. Having seen it, she knew she should return to the reception. But her footsteps dragged. It was so peaceful here, away from the festivities. She was in no hurry to return.

Noticing an intriguing plant in an alcove, she went to inspect it. Annegret was no gardener, but guessed it was some kind of lily. The dazzling cream flower was the size of a trumpet, and the jade-green dinner-plate-size leaves glistened as if painted. It looked too perfect to be real. She stretched out a hand.

"Don't touch that."

The order startled her so much that her hand closed reflexively around the plant's fleshy stem, and she gave a cry of shock as her palm was stung by what felt like hundreds of needles. She pulled away, feeling as if she had thrust her hand into a naked flame.

She looked up into a twin of the cobalt gaze she had been contemplating in the painting only a moment before. Except this time the eyes raking her belonged to Prince Maxim himself, and fierce glints sparked in their depths.

"I only wanted to see if the plant was real, Your Highness" she said, wishing she didn't feel like a child caught with her hand in the cookie jar. Assuming there were cookies that could make her hand feel as if it was on fire.

"The Janus lily is real, unfortunately," he said in a clipped tone that barely disguised a voice as deep and rich as hot chocolate. "When it's in flower, it's particularly dangerous. I'd ordered it moved from the alcove, but evidently the staff hadn't gotten around to it yet." His grim tone said someone would pay for the oversight.

"It's all right, really," she insisted, cradling her hand against her chest. As soon as the pain subsided, she would be fine. Less easy to deal with was the way her heart had started thundering with his approach.

Only shock, she assured herself, not sure how accurately. Up close, the prince was even more prepossessing than when she'd seen him outside the chapel. He was a few inches taller than Annegret herself, and she stood five-ten without heels. His hair was as dark and glossy as a night sky, and the hand he reached out to her looked strong and capable.

She had always had a thing for men's hands. The prince's might not appear work-worn, but neither did they look soft. His nails were clipped to a businesslike length and he wore a beaten-silver ring on the third finger of his right hand. Nothing on his left hand, but she already knew he was unmarried. Not that she cared.

"Let me take a look."

Before she could argue, he took her hand in his, uncurling her clenched fingers to reveal two red slashes across her palm where she had touched the plant stem. Each livid slash was impregnated with hundreds of hairlike filaments.

In as much pain as she was, she couldn't help noticing that his grasp was gentle, for all the anger in his expression. Her swift and very physical response caught her by surprise. She told herself it was because he was holding her hand and standing close enough for her to inhale a faint trace of his aftershave lotion—a blend of citrus and herbal scents that teased her nostrils.

"The Janus lily?" she queried, very much aware of needing the distraction. And not wholly because of the pain. "Wasn't Janus the Roman god of doorways and entrances?"

The prince nodded. "He was usually depicted wearing two faces."

She looked at the plant with renewed respect. "Like the lily, one beautiful, one dangerous."

"It's a Carramer native, one of the few that isn't benign," he explained. "They're only dangerous when in flower, and then only when touched."

"If you hadn't startled me, I wouldn't have touched it," she snapped, pain getting the better of her.

"If you hadn't been wandering where you shouldn't, I wouldn't have startled you," he countered mildly, but she heard a definite undercurrent of steel in his tone. Prince Maxim didn't take kindly to being crossed, she gathered.

Well, she didn't like being attacked by his feral plant, so they were even, she decided. She tugged her hand free, aware of a trace of regret accompanying the movement. "I wanted to see the *Champagne Pact*," she said tartly. "I didn't see any harm in it."

"This part of the castle is not open to the public, but you could have sought permission if you wished to view the painting."

"I hadn't planned that far ahead. The noise of the reception was giving me a headache, so I came looking for somewhere quieter. When I realized where I was, I decided to see if I could find the painting while I was here." Annoyance crept into her tone. She didn't like being on the defensive, especially since the prince was right. She shouldn't have trespassed, but she was darned if she was going to apologize. Her hand felt as if it was going to remind her of her folly for some time to come.

"Are you always so impulsive, Miss West?"

So he knew who she was. She felt a frisson of pleasure until it was overshadowed by common sense. Obviously, for a wedding held at a castle with royalty in attendance, everyone on the guest list would need security clearance. And he had probably memorized every name as a matter of course.

"Annegret," she offered. Then added, "Recklessness is an Australian trait." She shrugged, then wished she hadn't as a fresh burst of discomfort radiated along her forearm.

He saw the wince she couldn't quite conceal. "And now you're injured as a result. Let it be a lesson to you, Annegret. I'll have someone take you to the infirmary so your hand can be attended to.''

Furious at being dismissed so peremptorily, she stood her ground. ''I don't need medical attention. It's only a plant, for goodness sake. The effect should wear off in a few minutes.'' Maybe she was wrong about his strength, if he wanted to make this much fuss over a small mishap.

''Far from wearing off, the pain will escalate as the plant's toxin works its way into your bloodstream,'' he pointed out, sounding as if he rarely had to explain himself to anyone, and didn't appreciate the need now. ''If you aren't given an antidote soon, within a few hours you could become seriously ill.''

Spending her first vacation in years in a Carramer hospital was hardly appealing. And despite the evidence, she wasn't stupid. ''Very well, but I can't go anywhere until I've seen the bride and groom off,'' she insisted. ''I won't have their honeymoon spoiled by worrying about me.'' By now her friend should have finished changing into her going-away clothes. Annegret only hoped she hadn't already missed their departure.

The prince's eyebrows lifted as if her concern for her friends was a revelation. Whatever qualities he attributed to her evidently didn't include such consideration. ''Very well, but I'll accompany you, then see that you get to the doctor,'' he said.

''I won't run away as soon as you turn your back. I do have some sense.''

His glance suggested he wasn't convinced. ''You might also collapse without warning.''

She was starting to feel light-headed, but had put that down to his disturbing effect on her. The plant

might not be as deadly as he'd suggested, but there
was no point taking unnecessary risks. No more than
she had done by venturing into his private domain,
she amended inwardly.

"Okay, Your Highness," she said, with a soft ex-
halation of defeat. "Let's go back to the wedding. If
I collapse I'll depend on you to catch me."

His level gaze betrayed nothing, but she could
swear she heard him murmur, "It would be a pleasure."

Maxim knew he should be annoyed by her foray
into the family's apartments. Normally there would
have been at least two members of the Royal Protection Detail patrolling these corridors. Today, however,
one of their own was the groom, and most of the RPD
were attending the wedding. It didn't excuse the lapse
in security, and Maxim made a mental note to ensure
that someone paid for it. And that it didn't happen
again.

But he couldn't make himself feel as angry with
Annegret as he should be. He knew who she was, of
course. Even without his study of the guest list, her
crusade against hereditary monarchies conducted
through the TV series she produced was well known.
Her interest in the painting suggested she might be
considering doing a similar hatchet job on his own
family.

So he had absolutely no excuse for wanting to
spend more time with her than he had to. In spite of
her insistence on returning to the reception, it would
be a simple matter to summon a footman to escort
her, then take her to the infirmary before the plant's
toxin took full effect. But Maxim admired the way
she stood up to him. Not many people would have

dared. And he had to admit he was impressed by her insistence on putting her friends' well-being ahead of her own.

No one had ever died from touching the Janus lily, but the symptoms could be highly unpleasant. He was probably crazy letting her return to the function, but he had a feeling nothing short of gunpoint would change her mind, and that seemed a little extreme.

He released a taut breath and took her arm. ''Let's go.''

Holding her close to him, feeling her fight the plant's effects, produced mixed feelings of concern and something else. He told himself his interest in her was purely duty. Not good form to have her keel over on his doorstep. Certainly he would have done the same for anyone.

Anyone else, however, wouldn't have produced the heightened sense that warned him she was trouble. And not the kind that he could leave to the RPD. As she walked beside him, her willowy grace made him catch his breath. Few women could match him in height, but she came close, although she was slender enough to put hardly any pressure on his arm. Would sliding his arm all the way around her qualify as assisting her, or himself?

As they entered the grand hall where the reception was taking place, he felt her straighten, as if arming herself for a fight. It had to be with her increasing weakness, he concluded, and did slide his arm around her then, trying not to make his support too obvious. Or his own masculine response, for that matter.

Her fiery gaze told him she didn't like needing his help. ''Donna and Kevin should be here any minute now,'' she said.

He didn't miss the tremor she fought to conceal.

"You don't have to go through this. Nobody will notice if you're not around to catch the bouquet."

"I'll notice," she snapped.

He gave her an interested look. "Planning on catching it?"

"Never," she retorted in a fierce murmur.

His interest notched higher. "Never is a long time."

"When it comes to romantic love, it can't be long enough."

Keep her talking and her mind off her symptoms, he told himself. "Sounds like you've had a bad experience of romance."

"With respect, Your Highness, it's not really any of your business."

That settled that, he thought, her frankness rankling. It wasn't often anyone told him to back off, and he was surprised how little he liked it. Position going to your head? he asked himself. "You're right, it isn't," he conceded, striving for fairness. "I was only trying to distract you."

"A glass of wine might do a better job."

He shook his head. "I don't advise mixing alcohol with the poison in your system."

"You're probably right." Her breath whistled out. "What's keeping the lovebirds?"

He wondered the same thing, but for Annegret's sake, he said, "What's your connection to the couple?"

"Donna and I went to school together in Australia, then interned at the same TV studio. She came here on vacation and loved it so much she got a job with Carramer National Television."

"She and Kevin met when he accompanied me to a broadcast I was doing," the prince said.

Annegret looked surprise that he had noticed.

"It was hard to miss the sparks flying between them," Maxim explained. He had always wondered how it would feel to fall so hard and fast for someone. Not that he could afford to indulge his feelings. Better for his crown if he kept his distance.

The way he was doing now, came the disparaging thought. Annegret had moved closer and was leaning into his embrace. He didn't think she was aware of how her feathery blond hair brushed his cheek, bathing him in her delicate floral scent. Distance, he reminded himself.

Fortunately, Donna returned and dealt with the business of throwing her bouquet of tropical orchids, which was caught by one of the bridesmaids. Maxim and Annegret joined the throng wishing the couple well. He was thankful that everyone was too caught up in the moment to pay attention to the apparent closeness between the prince and one of the guests.

He felt a sense of relief when the couple drove away amid much laughter, ribald comments and a shower of rose petals.

"Now will you let me escort you to the infirmary?" he asked in a lowered tone.

Annegret's long lashes swept down over her forget-me-not blue eyes. "I don't think so."

She was swaying on her feet, leaning more heavily on his arm. "What do you mean? You're in no condition to go anywhere else," he insisted.

Her head moved in a weak arc. "I mean I don't think I can make it."

And she crumpled bonelessly into his arms.

Chapter Two

Ignoring the startled reaction of his sister, Princess Giselle, and the other wedding guests, Maxim began issuing orders. He refused an aide's offer to take the girl from him, and carried her through the corridors to the infirmary himself.

The castle had never seemed larger, he thought, aware of the slightness of the woman in his arms. She had reacted more swiftly to the effects of the Janus lily than anyone he'd ever known. If not for the feel of her heart thudding as he cradled her against his chest, he would have feared the worst.

Cursing himself for letting her delay seeking treatment, he gave a huge sigh of relief as he saw the doctor hurrying to meet him. A couple of medical staff followed with a stretcher.

Maxim surrendered his burden to them, aware of a strong reluctance to do so, although that made no sense. He knew she had brought the problem upon herself by trespassing in the royal apartments, but the condemnation he expected to feel wouldn't come. Instead, he felt only a gnawing anxiety that refused to dissipate.

The doctor was heading back toward the infirmary as Maxim briefed him on Annegret's encounter with the plant. When they reached the small but state-of-the-art facility, the antidote was produced within seconds.

Maxim felt his breath hiss out as the shot pierced Annegret's translucent skin. She stirred slightly as if feeling the sting. Perhaps she wasn't as deeply unconscious as she looked.

He found he was right. A few seconds later, her eyelids fluttered open. "That champagne really packs a kick," she murmured.

"So does the Janus lily," he reminded her gently.

Her eyes widened fully and she uncurled her hand in front of her face, inspecting the damage. "Does it hit everybody like that?"

He shook his head. "You must be particularly susceptible."

She lowered the hand, wincing when it pained her. "Remind me to stay away from them from now on."

He suspected she wouldn't need reminding. He turned to the doctor hovering at his shoulder. "How long before the antidote takes full effect?"

"Almost immediately, but because of the severity of the reaction, I advise keeping her here overnight for observation," the doctor said.

"I don't need to stay here. I'm fine, really." She struggled to sit up, then fell back against the pillow.

"So I see." Maxim addressed the doctor. "You have my permission to keep Miss West here as long as medically necessary."

''What about *my* permission?'' she asked tartly.

He folded his arms over his chest. ''After researching royalty for your documentaries, you should know that our word is invariably law.''

''You mean you ride roughshod over everybody because you can.''

He felt the corners of his mouth twitch, but kept his expression severe. ''Take it as you like, as long as you remain here.''

Her tantalizing mouth curved into a shaky smile, her defiance plain even when she must be feeling hellish. ''You realize you're confirming everything I've ever written about royalty?'' she asked softly.

Something snagged deep inside him, something more than admiration for her resilience. He resisted, wondering at the same time why he had to work so hard to do so. Some defiance of his own made him ask, ''Isn't that what you came to Carramer for?''

Anger flashed across her delicate features. She started to rise again, but he caught her shoulders and made her lie back, the ''something'' gaining strength as he touched her. He pulled his hands away as if singed.

When he straightened, she rocked her head to one side, avoiding his gaze. ''I came for Donna and Kevin's wedding.''

''And afterward?''

''A holiday.''

''And then?''

''All right, I had some thought of researching the Champagne Pact for my TV series.''

If she hadn't felt so terrible, Annegret knew she wouldn't have made the admission so readily. In her experience, people were more open if they didn't know her purpose, at least not at first. Ethics demanded that she identify herself at some point, but she hadn't lied to the prince. She *had* come to his country for Donna's sake.

As teenagers, she and Donna had sworn a childish oath to attend one another's weddings, imagining the handsome men who would one day sweep them off their feet. It had happened to Donna. For herself, Annegret wasn't sure it was ever going to. Prince Maxim might look like the magnificent specimen who had starred in her young dreams, but there the resemblance ended.

He crossed his arms over his broad chest. "Was that why you were snooping around, looking for the painting?"

She felt a flash of annoyance. "I wasn't snooping. No one stopped me from exploring, so I did."

"Unfortunately, I can't argue with you." His tone said the security lapse would be fixed so it wouldn't happen again. Heads would roll, she didn't doubt.

She didn't want it to be on her account. "Please don't hold your people responsible. I was the one at fault." Fleetingly, she wondered what her colleagues back home would say if they could hear their take-no-prisoners boss pleading with royalty.

His jaw hardened. "Nonetheless, they are responsible. However, since the same circumstances are unlikely to occur again, a reprimand should suffice."

She couldn't help herself. "It must be nice having so much power," she said dryly.

Thrusting his hands into his pockets, he observed, "The same might be said about you."

Given that she was the one lying flat on her back

on a hospital bed, even one as luxurious as this, she was puzzled, and said so.

He freed a hand to gesture elegantly. ''In your line of work, you reach millions of people with your belief that royalty is parasitical and unproductive.''

''I never said that.''

''You imply it every time you deal with the subject.''

Since it was what she believed, she couldn't argue. But his suggestion that she was one-sided in her handling of it stung more than the doctor's shot. ''I haven't had much luck convincing your peers to tell their side of the story.''

His gimlet gaze skewered her. ''Our side?''

She shifted restively, wishing their relative positions didn't put her at such a disadvantage. She settled for raising herself higher on the pillow. This time he didn't try to restrain her. Pity. ''There you go,'' she stated. ''You don't feel you have anything to prove, do you?''

''Not to you.''

''What about to the people who believe royalty is a relic of the past?''

''Preaching to the converted isn't the same as presenting a balanced viewpoint.''

She felt another flash of annoyance. He had a knack for touching sore spots, she'd noticed. That wasn't all he touched. The way he looked at her now, arrogant enough to prove his point and yet self-assured enough not to care, made her mouth go dry.

He wore a designer suit that skimmed the taut lines of his body. Handmade shoes polished to a mirror shine. Every hair was in place except for an errant curl escaping across his high forehead. That curl managed to make him look distractingly human, and she felt her hand stir, wanting to brush it back for him.

Resolutely she folded her fingers into a fist, burying it in the cashmere blanket she was resting on. "Are you accusing me of bias, Your Highness?"

"If the shoe fits."

Instead of the ire she expected to feel, satisfaction poured through her. "You realize what you've done? Now you have to give me an interview about the Champagne Pact." She played her trump card. "For balance."

He waited long enough for his silence to tell her he didn't have to do anything. "I'll consider it," he said finally. "In the meantime, you're to rest."

In truth, she needed to rest, but not here. "I don't have anything with me for an overnight stay."

"The staff will provide for your needs. Are you hungry?"

By rights her reaction to the plant venom should have killed her appetite. It hadn't. "A little," she admitted.

"I'll have a meal sent in to you."

This had gone far enough. "Now that your doctor's potion has done its job, I'd prefer to return to my hotel. I can rest there as easily as I can here. If it makes you feel better, you can provide a limo for me and a guard to make sure I get there."

The prince stepped closer, looming over her. "I have a better idea. You can spend the night in one of the guest suites, where the doctor will be on call."

It was an improvement on remaining where she was. "Very well."

"And dine with me."

"I wouldn't want to impose."

More than she had already done, his expression telegraphed more effectively than words. "Think nothing of it. I'll give the orders. When you're recovered enough to move, someone will escort you to me."

"I'm ready now." She swung her legs over the side of the bed, gripping the edge when the room swam around her. She didn't resist when he turned her shoulders and eased her back onto the pillow. "Well, maybe in a little while," she conceded, alarmed at feeling so weak.

He smiled. "Take all the time you need."

She let her eyes drift shut and the room slowly steadied. She heard the prince talking to the doctor, but felt too enervated to focus on what they were saying. She should be pleased with herself. She had gained something that had long eluded her—an honest-to-goodness prince who was willing to talk about royal life from the inside. If she could convince him to do it on camera, she would have an award-winning program.

Not a bad payoff for getting herself attacked by a carnivorous plant, she thought as her senses shut down.

She awoke feeling disoriented. Then memory flooded back. She sat up cautiously, but the room stayed steady. The doctor's potion and a long rest had done their work. "What time is it?" she asked the nurse who came in and checked a chart at the foot of her bed.

The woman dropped a hand to Annegret's wrist and counted beats before saying, "It's almost six."

Watching the nurse make a note on the chart, Annegret asked, "Six in the evening?"

The nurse replaced the chart. "You slept so soundly, Prince Maxim ordered that you not be disturbed."

Warmth infused Annegret. She had dreamed of Maxim standing over her, taking her hand. Had it only been a dream? "Was he here while I was asleep?"

"Twice. Would you like to freshen up? He had someone fetch your things from the Hotel de Merrisand. They'll be conveyed to your suite as soon as you are discharged from the infirmary."

Annegret was sure she hadn't told him the name of her hotel, and she most certainly hadn't given permission for anyone to go into her room. "How did he…"

"He is the prince," the nurse said, as if it explained everything.

Perhaps it did. At least Annegret could be thankful he hadn't gone to her hotel room himself. She found it easier to think·of a stranger touching her personal belongings, than to imagine Maxim doing it. It would be like having him touch her.

A shudder rippled through her, earning a concerned look from the nurse. "Are you sure you feel all right?"

Did heated skin and a light head count as all right? Aftereffects of her misadventure, Annegret assured herself. Nothing more. Certainly nothing that would justify fantasizing about Maxim.

"I'll be fine after I've showered and changed," she said, levering herself gingerly off the bed. Picking up her bag, she moved toward a doorway that she could see opened onto an adjoining bathroom.

Half an hour later, greatly refreshed and wearing a

white three-quarter-sleeve top and a black lace skirt, she emerged to find the bed tidied and the chart gone. On the pillow lay a single, long-stemmed red rose and a card bearing the royal crest. With her heart beating ridiculously fast, she picked up the card. "When you're ready, you'll be escorted to my apartment, although I believe you already know the way."

No signature. She held the rose to her face, breathing in the heady fragrance. If Maxim was trying to make a favorable impression, he was succeeding. It wouldn't influence how she portrayed him in her program, but she had to grant that His Royal Highness had style.

The corridors the uniformed footman led her along were steeped in shadows. Air-conditioning kept the temperature constant, so she must be imagining a chill from the thick stone walls, she told herself as she followed the servant. "What is Prince Maxim really like?" she asked the man.

"He is the prince."

The same answer the nurse had given her in the infirmary, as if it explained everything about him. "How does he spend his time?" she tried again.

"Administering the Merrisand Trust demands most of His Highness's time."

She knew that the trust raised millions of dollars to help children in need. "Surely the prince's staff do most of the work?" she prompted.

"The prince involves himself directly in the day-to-day running of the trust," the man said a little stiffly.

So he wasn't a figurehead. "But what is he really

like?'' she persisted, not sure that research was her
only motivation. "What are his hobbies?''

The man hesitated, as if unsure how much to reveal. Evidently deciding it wouldn't undermine the
stability of the crown, he said, "His Highness has a
passion for cartography—old maps.''

Her irritation rose. "I know what cartography is.''

"He is also a master astronomer. The Mount
Granet Observatory he founded is one of the largest
privately owned facilities in the southern hemisphere.''

The prince as a stargazer? The idea was almost too
romantic—and unsettling. *Because it doesn't fit your
preconceived notion of him?* she asked herself. Surely
she wasn't so prejudiced against royalty that she
couldn't deal with Maxim as a human being?

They had reached the royal apartments, so she was
about to find out.

The footman announced her as formally as if she
was making an entrance at a ball, but as soon as he
bowed his way out, Maxim came to her side, looking
relaxed and, she was forced to admit, devastatingly
attractive.

In contrast to his appearance at the wedding that
morning, he was casually dressed in charcoal pants
and an olive-green, open-necked shirt. The faintest
shadow darkened his chin, and light from the wall
sconces shot his ebony hair with silver glints. He was
going to age handsomely, she thought, gulping in air.

Not that he didn't look compelling enough now as
he took her hand and inspected the dressing covering
her palm. "How do you feel?''

"Refreshed after my rest, thank you, Your Highness.'' It had been the truth until he touched her. Now

she felt a shiver grip her. When he released her, she realized she had been holding her breath.

"Call me Maxim." He led the way through the apartment to a brightly lit kitchen. "Hungry?"

She looked around. "You're cooking?"

"Shouldn't I?"

"But I thought…"

"That I'd have servants bring us food on silver salvers? I do that, too. But occasionally I enjoy preparing something for myself. My sister says it keeps me humble."

Annegret rested her forearms on a countertop, glad of the barrier between them. She had been introduced to his sister, Princess Giselle, at the wedding. Both Maxim and his sister seemed unexpectedly approachable, but Annegret thought *humble* was stretching things. "Now, that I definitely have trouble picturing," she said.

His eyes sparkled. "Giselle agrees with you. Will ordinary do?"

He couldn't be that, either. Confusing messages assailed her. As a prince he was far more down-to-earth than she had expected. But neither could she deny the luxuriousness of their surroundings. He might be tossing ingredients into a soufflé dish, but he was doing it in state-of-the-art conditions in a castle. And the servants were a bellpull away in case the novelty wore off.

He left the cooking long enough to uncork a bottle of Pinot Noir. Her heightened senses made her acutely aware of the sound of the cork popping and the splash of the wine into crystal glasses. Aware of how deftly he handled the masculine chore. How strong his fingers looked wrapped around the delicate glass he handed to her.

When their fingers brushed, fire shot along her veins. Blaming the aftereffects of the Janus lily didn't quite work. Wine spattered onto the countertop as her hand shook.

"Still feeling some pain?" he asked in concern.

"A little," she lied, not wanting to admit the source of her discomfort, even to herself.

Maxim berated himself for keeping her standing in the kitchen while he indulged himself cooking for her. Showing off, he conceded. He had wanted to counter some of her prejudices with a demonstration of normality.

Who was he kidding? It wasn't hard to conjure up an impressive meal when the finest ingredients were provided and someone else did the cleaning up.

He wanted to believe he was teaching her a lesson. Instead, he was learning one. That to a point, she was right. He couldn't change who and what he was. So why not stop trying?

"Come through to the morning room," he said, taking her arm. He was reminded again of how slightly built she was for a woman who almost matched him in height.

"What about the soufflé?"

"It's almost ready for the oven. I'll ring for someone to take over here. You need to relax."

She didn't argue, proving his point. The morning room was his favorite room in the apartment, with floor-to-ceiling windows that wrapped around a table in the center. Presently the table was set for two. With the drapes drawn back to reveal the night sky in all its splendor, she would feel as if she was dining among the stars.

He heard her catch her breath, and shared a smile with her. "Beautiful, isn't it?" He wasn't sure he only meant the view.

"It's amazing. Do the stars always seem close enough to touch in Carramer?"

"Always." Pressing a hand to the small of her back, he moved her closer to the window. "The clarity of the air enables us to see far out into the universe."

Gesturing with his free hand, he said, "The reddish star blazing in the northeast is Arcturus. And that one is Regulus, the brightest star in the constellation Leo."

"It looks more like a sickle than a lion," she said to distract herself from the warmth of his hand against her back. "Your Regulus looks like the handle, with the blade hanging below it."

"Very perceptive," he agreed. "Our ancestors used to think the stars were holes in the night to let the light of heaven pass through."

She'd been told that the prince was a keen astronomer. She hadn't expected him to be a poet, as well. "It's a beautiful thought, however unscientific," she observed.

He pulled out a chair for her where she could continue to watch the stars, then left her long enough to issue orders. By the time she'd drunk a little of the excellent wine, a servant had brought their meal, served them efficiently, then left them alone. Also according to orders.

Whether it was due to the stars, the meal or his efforts to help her relax, Maxim was gratified to see some color return to her cheeks. "Feeling better now?"

"Much, thank you." There was no reason to assume his nearness was the cause. She had eaten very little at the wedding, so her blood sugar had probably been in her boots. The soufflé had melted in her mouth. "It's kind of you to be so concerned."

He lifted his wineglass. "Kindness has nothing to do with it."

"Then what?"

"Perhaps a wish to show you a more flattering side of royalty you can share with your television viewers in the future."

"Why?"

He'd been asking himself the same thing. He settled for honesty. "I may be a prince, but I'm also a man. I find you very attractive, Annegret."

This time he had no doubt that her heightened color was his doing. She was speechless, he saw, and suspected it wasn't a condition she experienced often.

She recovered quickly. "You must know the feeling is mutual."

Warmth surged through him. Was it to be so simple, then? The Champagne Pact might bind him to marry a woman of royal blood, but it didn't stop him from enjoying the company of a commoner. That he might be playing with fire, he also recognized. Annegret struck him as an all-or-nothing sort of woman.

He replenished their glasses, deciding to test his theory. "Then all that remains is to decide what we're going to do about it."

Chapter Three

Annegret's heart started to pound, and her palms felt damp, the right one throbbing under the dressing. One glass of wine didn't justify blurting out that she was attracted to him, even if it was true.

Trying to deny it now would only get her in deeper, so she said, "We're not going to do anything. At least I'm not."

He toyed with the stem of his glass. "Why not?"

"If it wasn't for the Janus lily, I would be safely back at my hotel by now, and there would be nothing to discuss."

"You don't feel safe here?"

He was far too quick. "I didn't mean safe as in *safe*. I meant we wouldn't be having this conversation."

His eyes gleamed as if he knew perfectly well that she had been referring to emotional safety. "However, we are having it and I, for one, have no regrets."

She had plenty. If she had known he was interested

in her, she would have insisted on returning to her hotel instead of accepting his offer to stay at the palace.

But you did know, a small inner voice insisted. She had known it the moment he set eyes on her. Her experience with the male of the species may have been limited to a few carefully chosen encounters, but she knew enough to recognize when a man found her appealing. The fact that she was now alone with Maxim in his private quarters confirmed her instinctive assessment.

So why had she agreed? She could have spent the night in the infirmary as the doctor had recommended, or arranged to be taken back to her hotel. Yet here she was, hackles rising at hearing the prince say what she had suspected all along. She couldn't have it both ways. "I don't regret accepting your invitation, but that's as far as I intend to go," she said.

"Because of who I am?"

They were interrupted by a servant clearing away their plates and placing slices of featherlight lemon gâteau on fine china in front of them. When the servant had gone, Annegret toyed with her dessert. "I make it a point never to get involved with titled men."

"Aren't you getting ahead of yourself? Attraction can also lead to friendship."

She felt herself flushing. As a teenager, she'd imagined her biological father saying something similar to her mother. Charming her with his aristocratic ways until Debra West was hopelessly in love. Then abandoning her without a backward glance. Annegret had no intention of letting that happen to her.

Bad enough that she had come close with Brett

Colton. His father, the owner of the network that owned her show, was the nearest thing Australia had to royalty. Her pedigree, or lack of one, was the reason his father had disapproved of her. Brett hadn't admitted it outright, but he hadn't denied it when she asked if that was the reason he had ended their relationship.

Brett had known about her mother's liaison with the prince's equerry. Would things have been different if he had married her mother? Since he hadn't, and since Annegret had wanted Brett to love her for herself rather than for her family background, she had accepted the situation with as much poise as possible. She had waited until she was alone to give way to tears over the injustice of being judged on a factor so far out of her control.

In future she would think twice about becoming involved with a man—especially one so far out of her own social league. And if anyone had a problem with her background, she'd make sure to find out before her heart became involved.

Still, she hadn't expected to find herself enjoying a private dinner with Brett's counterpart here. "Have you considered that I might use a friendship against you, Your Highness?" she asked the prince.

He acknowledged her use of his title with a slight nod. "In my position, that's always a possibility."

"Because you'd do the same thing yourself?" She didn't really believe it, but she wanted to see his reaction. For her TV show, of course.

He put his dessert fork down. "I don't know who you're mixing me up with, Annegret, but that's not the way I operate."

"Yet you admit to being attracted to me, knowing

that the terms of the Champagne Pact mean nothing can come of it.''

"It doesn't stop me from having friends, or feelings.''

"Only from doing anything about them unless the woman has blue blood.'' Abandoning any pretense to herself that the show was the reason she wanted Maxim to know where she stood, she decided to put all her cards on the table. See how fast Maxim lost his desire for her friendship then. "You may as well know that my biological father was merely a courtier to the prince of Ehrenberg.'' She stretched her arm out on the pristine tablecloth, the delicate veins appearing close to the surface in the glow of candlelight. "See? Not a trace of blue blood.''

Maxim slid his index finger over her upturned wrist, resting it a moment on her fluttering pulse. He suspected his own was just as fast. He told himself it was due to her confession that she hadn't a trace of royal blood. Not that he had any intention of taking his interest in her further than friendship, he thought, before his hormones could kick in full strength. He suspected there was something else she wasn't telling him.

"It's a myth that royal blood is blue,'' he said, far more calmly than he felt.

"So I'm told,'' she stated flatly, withdrawing her arm. "It hardly matters, since my father never acknowledged my existence. He was equerry to Prince Frederick, Ehrenberg's ambassador to Australia. My mother met my father when she worked at the embassy as a member of the diplomatic service. Soon after, she learned that she was pregnant, the prince was recalled to his country and my father went with him. She never heard from him again.''

Annegret's matter-of-fact tone couldn't quite conceal the hurt he heard in her voice. She might like to be seen as tough, but she wasn't, Maxim would bet on it. The hurt sounded raw enough to be on her own account, as well as her mother's. Had some man left Annegret herself in the lurch, awakening echoes of her mother's bitter experience?

It hardly mattered to him, Maxim assured himself. He was attracted to her, but it didn't mean he had to do anything about it beyond spending this evening in her company. For her sake and his own, he couldn't afford to. The evening was probably a mistake, too, although he couldn't make himself believe it.

''Why are you telling me this?'' he asked.

Her finger traced patterns on the linen tablecloth. ''If we're going to work together, you're entitled to know something of my background.''

She expected him to reject her because of what had happened between her mother and father, he saw with sudden insight.

''You'd be surprised how much I already know,'' he admitted, earning a raised eyebrow and a sudden wariness in her gaze. ''You must have expected my security people to check out everyone on today's guest list?''

He could almost hear her thoughts whirring, hear her thinking, *You're attracted to me, knowing who and what I am?* She obviously didn't know that royal history, even Carramer's, was littered with heirs with far less claim to blue blood than her own.

''Ehrenberg has been closed to outsiders for almost

three decades. Perhaps leaving your mother wasn't your father's choice,'' he suggested.

She nodded. ''I considered that, but the revolution didn't take place until a month after I was born— plenty of time for him to at least get in touch. Give my mother his regrets. He didn't bother.''

Maxim couldn't explain that himself, unless her father was as amoral as Annegret believed. The prince didn't care to be compared with such a man. ''It doesn't mean everyone connected with royalty is the same.''

She pushed her half-finished dessert aside and reached for some ice water. ''The headlines, and my own research for the program, suggest differently.''

''Affairs make better headlines than happy marriages.''

Unable to refute that, she stared into the glass. ''True. My viewers enjoy scandal as much as anyone.''

''Are you hoping to unearth some scandal about the royal house of Carramer?''

Her head lifted and her gaze blazed a challenge at him. ''I don't go looking for it, if that's what you're suggesting. I also report good news when I find it.'' Her tone suggested she rarely did.

''Then perhaps I can help you find some.''

''You've already promised me an interview.'' He hadn't in so many words, but Annegret couldn't see any benefit in pointing that out. If he really wanted her to report objectively on his family, it was in his own best interests to cooperate.

He took a sip of wine. ''I'm thinking of more than an interview. You're familiar with the work of the Merrisand Trust?''

"It's the charity you administer that raises funds to help underprivileged children and their families," she said, fighting a sense of disappointment. If he was going to suggest she do a puff piece on his charity, she wasn't interested. Not because she didn't want to report good news, but because the trust had already been the subject of several documentaries. Her series was successful because she delved beneath the surface of her subjects.

"Next week, I'm launching a new ship that will provide cruises for the trust's clients," he said.

"Good for you."

Although she spoke under her breath, he frowned as if he'd heard. "The vessel was built and placed at the disposal of the trust by the Soral Shipping Line."

This time her flicker of interest was genuine. "Owned by the family who stand to inherit your crown under the terms of the Champagne Pact?"

The prince nodded. "Chad Soral is the head of the shipping line and the current claimant, if it should come to that. He'll be presenting the vessel to the trust."

Suspicion slid up her spine. "Why would you allow me to meet your rival?"

"Balance," he reminded her imperturbably, and picked up his dessert fork.

Taking her cue from him, she did the same. The cumulative effect of the acidic dessert was dizzying to her senses. Nothing to do with the way Maxim was regarding her as his lips closed around a mouthful of his own dessert.

Her heart kicked in irritating contradiction. She wished he didn't keep this room so warm, although she had only begun to notice the fact in the last few

seconds. It had to be because she was excited at the
prospect of securing interviews with the prince *and*
his rival, she assured herself.

"Do you think Chad will agree to appear on my
show?" she asked.

Watching her across the table, Maxim thought if
she fluttered those impossibly long lashes at Chad the
way she was doing now, he would probably agree to
anything she asked of him. Max himself was tempted,
and he wasn't half the ladies' man that Chad was. Of
course, he wasn't hampered by the limitations that
ruled Max. Chad could marry anyone he wished without consequences.

Max knew he had resented this aspect of his rival's
life since they were at university together. In those
days Max had fallen heavily for one woman in particular, the daughter of one of the lecturers, but Max
had forced himself to grit his teeth and keep silent
while Chad charmed her into dating him.

Seeing the way Max had looked at her, Chad had
magnanimously offered to get out of their way. He
could afford to, Max remembered thinking. If anything came of the relationship, the crown would become Chad's. The man couldn't lose. The prince had
salvaged his self-respect by pretending to have no interest in the young woman. Curiously enough, Chad
had also lost interest in her soon afterward.

Max wondered if Chad knew how tempted he had
been to abdicate his responsibilities then and there
and follow his heart. He hadn't, of course. No matter
what the personal cost, Maxim refused to go down in
history as the last de Marigny to wear the crown of
Taures.

Was history about to repeat itself now? Why had

he tempted fate by suggesting that Annegret meet Chad? Getting in first before he could be hurt a second time? That made her far more important to Maxim than he wanted her to be.

"You'll have to ask Chad about an interview," the prince said, adding caustically, "He isn't known for his shyness."

She nodded in acknowledgment. "So I've heard." Because she knew there had to be more, she said, "What do you get out of taking me along? Besides balanced reporting, of course."

"Isn't your company sufficient reason?"

Instant denial caught her by surprise. Not because she didn't know her own worth, but because she suspected *he* didn't. Not yet. In her experience, men like him operated according to their own agenda. Seduction was no more than a side dish accompanying the main banquet, and though her toes curled inside her shoes at the thought, she made herself ask what else he wanted from her.

As she voiced the question, the prince's dark eyebrows lifted. "Very well, I hope to employ your skills as a filmmaker to benefit the Merrisand Trust."

She refused to acknowledge the stabbing sensation as disappointment. It was no more than she had suspected. "I don't do corporate work," she stated.

"Not even in exchange for an exclusive story on the Champagne Pact?"

The feeling of being cheated deepened. "Blackmail, Your Highness?"

"Call it a quid pro quo, an even exchange of favors."

"The trust has been documented on film several times already."

"Not for many years, and not by you."

She crumpled her linen napkin on the table. "How do you know I'd do a good job?"

"I've studied your work. I find it original and insightful."

The thought of him demanding a private screening of her shows provoked a warm glow she resisted. "Even though I lack balance?"

"You've admitted you're biased on the subject of royalty. You may change your opinion once you've seen something of royal life from the inside."

Her opinion wouldn't change, as he would soon find out. The certainty didn't stop her from asking, "What do you have in mind?"

The question betrayed more interest than she intended, and she saw his eyes take on a speculative gleam. "Considering my proposition, Annegret?"

"I don't have much choice, if I want a story on the Champagne Pact."

"We always have choices," he reminded her smoothly. "In spite of how it might sound, this isn't blackmail. Under duress, you're unlikely to give me the result I want."

"Which is?"

His brow furrowed with thought. "There are some who feel that charitable trusts such as Merrisand are an anachronism in the modern world."

Like royalty, she heard, although he didn't say it. Unwillingly, she acknowledged a frisson of excitement creeping through her. "You want to show that they still have a place," she suggested.

He nodded. "Precisely. I want you to make a documentary piece tracing the trust's evolution from dispenser of royal favors to a modern-day force making the world a better place.''

He really believed that was what he was doing, she thought, noting the fervor in his words and expression. He was a man of passion, as she'd suspected. That it was directed toward helping the less fortunate was more disturbing.

Because it argues with your preconceptions about him? she asked herself. She shook off the question, channeling her mind into more practical areas. ''I don't have time to get a crew together before the launch.''

''Nor do I expect it. Consider the cruise as a chance to develop your ideas about where the project might go. We'll discuss your plans and formalize arrangements afterward.''

He was talking about this as a done deal, she noticed, well aware that she was already thinking along similar lines. She was torn between annoyance at the smooth way he had manipulated her into doing his bidding, and the thrill of meeting his challenge.

How had he managed it? *He is the prince,* she recalled the nurse at the infirmary saying, echoed later by one of his footmen. Was it really so simple? Were certain people gifted with skills and abilities beyond the ordinary, or was she in danger of becoming as much a victim of the royal mystique as her mother had been?

The thought made her bristle. ''How long is this cruise supposed to last?'' she asked, more roughly than she'd intended.

He didn't seem to notice as he finished his dessert and folded his napkin. ''I'll be aboard for two nights.

The inaugural cruise lasts for a week, so you can stay on as long as you wish.''

She resisted the urge to gulp. Two nights aboard a cruise vessel with the prince was more than she had bargained for. She had already taken a dinner cruise on Merrisand's Summer Harbor and knew how seductive the moonlight and the waves could be. Add Maxim to the mix...

Stop it, she ordered herself. His proposal ensured that she would have plenty to keep her occupied while she was on board. In any case the prince would be occupied with his duties and the official guests such an occasion invariably involved. She would be lucky to see him for more than a few minutes each day. And that wouldn't bother her.

For some time now, rumors had floated around the network that her show might be replaced in the schedule next season. The cruise would provide her with the perfect opportunity to line up a blockbuster opening show to ensure that the series was renewed. In addition, Maxim had just handed her a plum assignment that most producers would give their eyeteeth to be offered. Nothing else mattered to her.

She blotted her mouth with the snowy napkin, determined to ignore the riot of sensations pouring through her. This was business. Never mind that she would be cruising the blue waters around Merrisand with the most fascinating man she had met in a long time. Hadn't she already learned the folly of such thinking?

''Coffee?'' he invited.

Her eyelids were drooping, the aftereffects of the plant sting, she assumed. ''No, thank you. I'd prefer to go to bed.''

Unfortunate phrasing, she realized when she saw his interest sharpen. Then she saw something stranger. He clamped down on the response with a visible effort. She should be grateful, she knew. Contrarily, she wasn't.

"I'll have someone escort you to your suite," he said. "Your overnight bag is already there. If you need anything else, you have only to ring for it."

What she needed, a servant would unlikely be able to provide, she thought, aware of feeling cheated by the prince's obvious resistance to her. Had she expected him to swoon at her feet? It would have made a good story for her program, she thought, striving for humor. TV Producer Brings down Royal House.

It was also so far from possibility that she was wasting her time thinking about it, she told herself as she got to her feet and thanked the prince for dinner.

Bending slightly from the waist, he took her hand and lifted it to his lips, his gaze never leaving hers.

It would take more than kissing her hand to change her opinion of royalty, but the assurance didn't prevent a medley of sensations from shivering along her spine as his lips brushed her heated skin.

Better get ahold of herself before the cruise, she decided. To do her job she needed to be calm and in control. At the moment, with Maxim's fingers tangled with hers, she was neither, and the teasing light in his eyes told her he was well aware of the fact. And enjoying every minute of it.

Chapter Four

Annegret had always loved to run. She didn't run away from anything in particular. As a child, she had preferred to stand and fight even when a bully was twice her size. And they often were. For some years, it had been her misfortune to be the only child in her class lacking a father. These days one-parent families were so common that nobody thought twice about it, but twenty years ago she had been an oddity, either pitied or teased until she had bloodied a few noses to demonstrate that she didn't need a father to stand up for her. She could do it for herself. There was freedom in running.

As an adult, running was her indulgence, a chance to stretch herself physically while her thoughts took flight on their own.

As a teenager she had thought of becoming an athlete. Speed was on her side. What she lacked was focus. She hadn't needed her high school coach to point out that a true athlete concentrated solely on the task at hand. Annegret had been too easily distracted by what was going on around her. When she had no explanation for someone's behavior, she would make up her own story, almost unconsciously figuring out the best angles from which to tell it.

In short, she had a producer's mind in a runner's body.

It wasn't a bad combination, she had decided. Although her coach had despaired of cajoling Olympian performances out of her, she had discovered that running helped her to cut through the clamor of everyday living to the heart of her problems.

She was hoping to find that clarity now. Two days of living at the castle had brought her no closer to deciding what to do about Maxim's proposal. Interviewing him and his rival for her show was one thing. Agreeing to live and work in Merrisand while she documented the work of the trust was quite another.

It wasn't that she had any trouble imagining herself staying in Carramer. Who wouldn't enjoy living in a place made up of equal parts tropical rain forest and island paradise?

She refused to allow that Maxim himself was the problem. Since he'd invited her to stay at the castle until the cruise, she'd only seen him at dinner and then in the company of other guests, so their exchanges had remained superficial.

Once or twice she'd intercepted his heated gaze across the room and felt her internal temperature rise in response. But there had been no chance for a private moment, and she told herself she was glad.

He wasn't free to pursue whatever they'd agreed had sparked between them. And she wasn't interested in the kind of dalliance that led nowhere except to heartache. She'd broken her own rule with Brett Colton and look where that had gotten her. Rejected by his father as not good enough for his son, she could only imagine how much worse it would feel being rejected by a whole country. She wasn't that much of a masochist.

In any case, the prince had offered her a job, not a marriage proposal, she reminded herself. She didn't want it any other way.

Almost in spite of herself, she had been intrigued by the challenge of giving her own filmic twist to the story of the Merrisand Trust. When she wasn't enjoying the luxury of being waited on hand and foot, she had spent her time in the castle's extensive library, taking notes and playing with ideas.

Her hand had almost entirely healed since her encounter with the Janus lily. A red patch on her palm was almost the only remaining sign of the injury, and she had been careful to give the plant a wide berth since then. Maxim had kept his promise to have the flowering version moved from the alcove near the painting, she had noticed when she'd returned to study it afresh yesterday.

With a perfect right to be there this time, she had spent almost an hour in front of the painting, trying to imagine the Soral family's state of mind when they'd imposed the conditions of the pact on their prince. And what had moved him to accept, binding the males in his family to almost two hundred years of emotional torment. Women couldn't inherit the Taures crown, or no doubt they would have suffered under the pact as well.

Knowing how it felt to have love snatched away, she empathized with the successive generations of princes who had been forced to choose between their heart's desire and their crown. The physical resemblance between Maxim and his ancestor made it all too easy to imagine him as a modern-day Romeo, kept from his Juliet by the constraints of history.

There was no Juliet, she chided herself. From what she had seen and read, Maxim was too strong a man to let himself be sidetracked by romantic love. He could, as he'd said, permit himself to have friends and feelings. But there it would end.

He is the prince. Strange how often that phrase came back to her, with its overtones of duty and nobility. Did he ever tire of being noble? Or dream of riding off into one of Carramer's spectacular sunsets with the love of his life?

Irritated with herself, she reined in her runaway thoughts. There were times when an overheated imagination was a liability. Such as when she started picturing herself riding off into the sunset with him. He had asked for a documentary, not a romantic fantasy, and he certainly wasn't auditioning her for a lead role. Even if he might have done, she wouldn't be interested, would she?

As her long legs devoured the heated sand of Merrisand beach, she dismissed the disturbing thought, distracting herself with the pleasure of filling her lungs with the crystalline air. She had never had a private beach all to herself before.

Before he and Donna were married, Kevin Jordan had shown Annegret the ribbon of golden sand that was part of the Merrisand Castle grounds. It was only a short drive from the castle itself, and Annegret had admired it without imagining she would soon have the run of it, literally.

This morning she had asked one of Prince Maxim's security people if there was a beach where she could run, and they had recommended this place, even providing a car and driver to ferry her from the castle. As the prince's guest, it seemed she had the freedom of the royal enclaves.

She could get used to this life, she thought. When she was shown to her suite two nights before, she had found her meager possessions unpacked and hanging in lonely splendor in the vast walk-in closet. She had been glad there was no one to see her giggling like a schoolgirl as she explored the double bedroom complete with en suite bathroom, and spacious living room with a semicircular terrace opening off it.

Unable to resist, she had called her mother from the telephone in the bathroom. When she heard where her daughter was, Debra West had sounded slightly bemused, but glad that Annegret was so obviously enjoying herself.

The suite even had a well-equipped kitchen area where she could prepare food if she wanted to. Not that she needed any such thing as long as there were servants to awaken her with a tray of freshly brewed coffee and pastries each morning. At home, she usually breakfasted on cereals and fresh fruit, but the featherlight pastries had proved so tempting that on her first morning here she had polished them off, mopping up every last crumb with a moistened finger before getting out of bed. As penance, she had skipped the pastries this morning in favor of running off the calories.

If only Brett Colton could see her now, she thought. Would his father be so quick to dismiss her potential if he knew she was living in a castle, in quarters fit for a princess?

Probably.

Her steps faltered as she reminded herself that living like a princess didn't make her one, any more than Prince Maxim's attempt to cook dinner for her on her first night at the castle made him an ordinary man.

They were what they were. She wasn't ashamed of what she was, or particularly envious of Maxim. As she had assured her mother, she was perfectly capable of enjoying the pleasures of castle life while she could, before returning to her own reality.

With that assurance, Annegret found her rhythm again, lengthening her stride until she felt as if she were flying over the sand. If she had to, she could maintain this pace for miles.

A shadow fell across her and her steps almost faltered again as Maxim fell into stride beside her. "Mind if I join you?"

She kept her pace even with an effort. "It's your beach, Your Highness."

"Right now it looks as if you own it. You run very well."

He wasn't doing so badly himself, she noticed. He must have warmed up farther down the beach before putting on a burst of speed to catch up with her. Now he kept pace with her effortlessly, his breathing as deep and even as her own.

"So do you," she conceded. "Do you make a habit of this?"

He shook a lock of hair out of his eyes. "As many mornings as I can. When I travel, I try to run wherever I am, although it tends to give my security people heart failure."

She cast a glance over her shoulder, noting the two men forging along in the prince's wake. They were a few dozen yards behind and looked as if they would prefer to be just about anywhere else. "Maybe you should ask for more athletic bodyguards," she said with a grin.

His answering smile was like the sun coming out. "That wouldn't be half as much fun. Besides, they need this more than I do."

She couldn't argue with that. Clad in black running shorts trimmed with white stripes, and a black polo shirt, the prince looked like a professional athlete. His legs could have done a Michelangelo sculpture proud, every muscle and sinew delineated by his powerful movements. He ran close enough beside her to reveal the scattering of dark hair on his olive-toned skin.

Having someone to pace her made a welcome change, she found, and she speeded up without conscious thought. He matched her stride for stride, until the bodyguards were left a long way behind.

"This can't be good for your security," she said, concern overtaking the heady exhilaration of the run.

The prince glanced back, then at her. "If I let myself worry too much about my safety, I'd never step outside the castle walls."

She slowed to a comfortable jog. "All the same, perhaps we should let them catch up." The prince's cavalier attitude toward his own security troubled her more than she wanted to admit.

Something in her tone alerted him. "Worried about me, Annegret?"

Admitting it would be far too revealing, so she shook her head. "Given the number of staff at your beck and call, that would be redundant, wouldn't it?"

He turned around, jogging backward so he could look at her. "Do I hear a criticism of royal life?"

A shrug lifted her narrow shoulders. "You know I'm not a fan."

He turned back and began to pace her again. "Not even of being spoiled yourself?"

Had the royal treatment been a setup to prove she had as much taste for luxury as the next person? The limo ride to the private beach? The masseuse he'd sent to her suite the previous morning? She felt the start of a guilty flush. She hadn't exactly rejected any of them. "I can take it or leave it." The dismissal didn't sound particularly convincing even to her own ears. "I don't exactly live in penury back in Australia," she added in her own defense.

She steered toward a group of rocks rising like sentinels out of the sand. Reaching them, she flopped down on an armchair-shaped one, waiting for her breathing to steady. That it took longer than usual, she blamed on Maxim settling himself on a rock alongside her.

"Where exactly is Kincumber? If I have the pronunciation right," Maxim asked.

The resonant way he said the name of her hometown made it sound like some impossibly beautiful, exotic destination. "Close enough," she said, flushing even more as she realized how easily he influenced her feelings. She cleared her throat self-consciously. "It's a village about an hour's drive north of Sydney on the Central Coast of New South Wales. My cottage is a couple of streets back from a popular fishing beach where I run when I'm not away filming." She and the bank shared ownership of the cottage, but she didn't expect Maxim to have much experience with the concept of a mortgage, so she saw no reason to mention it.

The prince gestured around them. "Like this?"

"It's beautiful in its own way, but I don't usually have it all to myself."

He braced a foot against the rock and rested his forearms on his upraised knee. "What about the cottage? Do you have that all to yourself?"

She felt her gaze turn bleak. Given Brett's wealthy background, she had never expected him to move in with her, but had been hurt when he referred to her "beach shack," quashing some of her excitement at finally having her own place. Be it ever so humble, she had told him, not bothering to hide her indignation. He hadn't understood.

"Didn't your background check tell you all about me?" she asked the prince.

He shook his head. "Only whether or not you're a security risk."

"And am I?" she couldn't resist asking.

Only to his peace of mind, Maxim thought. "The RPD didn't think so. At least there were no red flags on your file."

He saw her curiosity sharpen. "Red flags?"

"Warnings about subversive activities in your own country that you might want to bring to Carramer."

She gave a brittle laugh. "I'm disappointed that they don't consider my show subversive enough. I really work at that."

"Perhaps they sense that it's primarily meant to entertain," he observed. "They'd be more concerned if your show was overtly supportive of the monarchy, while you attended rallies or published propaganda with a different message."

"No wonder they were disappointed. I have no hidden agenda." Perhaps if she had, the series wouldn't be in danger of cancellation because of tightening budgets at the TV station, but she didn't tell him that. Evidently it was a detail his security checks hadn't revealed.

She didn't know whether to be glad or sorry. It would have been easier if Maxim already knew everything there was to know about her. Finding that he didn't when she'd expected him to made her uncomfortable. It couldn't be because of the risk that he'd be disappointed by what he finally learned. So why did she care?

The security men had caught up with their prince and had stationed themselves in the shade near the tree line, their relaxed posture suggesting they were happy not to be on the move for the moment.

Her gaze flickered from them back to Maxim. He behaved as if his staff weren't even there, while she found the constant observation unnerving. Maybe you had to grow up with servants before they became invisible to you. Tools rather than people. As she was to the prince, she reminded herself.

The timely thought made her scramble to her feet. "I'm cooling down. Time to get moving again."

He uncoiled from the rock. "Race you back to the cars."

Her self-imposed reminder of her place in Maxim's scheme of things had stung so sharply that movement came as a welcome antidote. "You're on. The loser buys dinner tonight."

Without waiting for his acknowledgment, she started back the way they'd come, flying across the sand in graceful strides. ▬

Maxim watched her go, aware that he was indulging himself as much as giving her a head start. Not that she needed one. She was as fluid and fleet as one of Carramer's native sun deer. He was going to have his work cut out to catch up. He signaled to his bodyguards to follow, then took off after her.

He had been right about her speed. But he was no tortoise himself, and was soon pounding down the beach close on her heels. Her breathing sounded fast but steady, the efficient air use of the long-distance runner. He fell into step beside her, grinning as he stated, "I should warn you, I have expensive tastes."

She gulped air. "Did I mention that my favorite restaurant is in Noumea?"

"You haven't won yet."

Without warning she put on a sudden spurt, and he found himself working hard just to keep up, much less pull ahead of her. The sensation of genuine challenge was so novel that he almost forgot how much he hated to lose.

Muscles burning, Annegret forced herself through sheer contrariness to keep going. Mentally she reached for the trance that normally carried her beyond the limits of her endurance, into a zone where she could keep up a steady pace for hours. This time the zone wasn't within her reach.

Sweat soaked her shorts and T-shirt and splashed into her eyes. She dashed it away, not sure why winning was so important to her, only knowing that it was. Protocol probably demanded that she let the prince beat her to the finish line—a stand of ironwood trees where she could see sunlight glinting off their cars. But stubbornness was her middle name. She had never willingly lost a race in her life, and wasn't about to start now. That she might be trying to prove something to herself as much as to Maxim, she refused to think about.

The sand that had felt so yielding when she started running now felt like concrete under her pounding feet. The impact rebounded through her like blows. She was more of an endurance runner than a sprinter, and Maxim was pushing her to her limits.

So be it. She ignored the ache in her muscles and ran on, aware that she was moving faster than she'd ever done.

It wasn't enough. Whenever she spared a breath to glance around, he was at her side as if glued there. Not pulling ahead, she was gratified to notice, but not falling behind, either. In fact, she would have sworn he had speed in reserve and was taunting her by keeping pace with her.

"Don't you dare do me any favors," she snapped, provoked beyond endurance.

"Such as letting you win?"

He was trying to psych her out, she recognized, and it was close to working. Now if she reached the trees ahead of him, she would never know whether he had gone easy on her or if she had won fair and square.

There was only one solution. She followed his lead and kept pace with him, stride for stride. It wasn't easy, because his legs were longer and he had a slight height advantage. But she was nothing if not determined, as Maxim was about to find out.

She crossed the imaginary finish line at the exact moment he did, timing her footfall to impact on the grass edging the sand as if they were participating in a three-legged race.

Bending at the waist, she braced her hands on her

knees and waited for her breathing to slow. When it did, she looked up at him. "Good race."

"Fixed race," he said, glaring at her.

"Because you didn't win?"

"Because you weren't trying to win. Did you go for a tie out of some crazy notion that it isn't good form to beat royalty?"

So he had guessed what she was doing. "I thought you were the one trying to do me a favor."

He didn't deny it, she noticed, but held out his hand. "Next time we race flat out or not at all. Deal?"

When she gripped his hand it felt scorchingly hot and as damp as her own. "Deal." Her heartbeat still hadn't returned to normal—a product of the exertion or the prince's nearness?

Both were playing havoc with her system, but she suspected that the prince's strong fingers curled around hers had more to do with the unevenness of her breathing and the pounding in her chest. "So dinner's off?" she said, more casually than she felt.

A lock of damp hair fell across his forehead as he shook his head. "Uh-uh. I consider you won on handicap, so your pick it is."

While filming in Noumea she had fallen in love with a particular restaurant, but had been joking when she'd suggested going there. "We can't, it's in another country."

Unperturbed, he asked, "What's special about this place?"

She struggled to think. "Poisson Arlequin has cave walls with enormous fish tanks set into them. Sharks swim right past your table so it feels as if you're dining under the sea."

His eyes brightened with recognition. "I know it.

I'll have a helicopter standing by at six, and reservations for eight. Unless you want to concede that I won.''

Her natural competitiveness wouldn't permit it. Or was it simply the desire to spend an evening in his company, against all common sense? "I'll be ready at six," she assured him.

Chapter Five

Only a prince could casually discuss flying to another country for dinner, she mused as she got ready that evening. Some women would think it romantic. They wouldn't see that the notion was typical of royal extravagance. Annegret was determined not to be seduced by the glamor and excitement of it. Of him.

With a passport but no visa for Noumea, she couldn't go there with him even had she wanted to, and she didn't. On the other hand, maybe royalty didn't need such niceties. The spark of amusement in his expression when he'd said she'd won was enough to make her wonder what he really had in mind for tonight.

Deciding she would find out soon enough, she showered and changed into the one fancy dress in her travel wardrobe, a silk shantung designer black shift split to the thigh at both sides. High-heeled leather slides felt cool on her bare feet. A pair of coral earrings she'd bought at a market in Merrisand completed the outfit.

In the shower she had washed her short-cropped hair. Now she fluffed it out with her fingers. A glance in the mirror told her it needed no further attention. She was aiming for understated elegance. She didn't want Maxim thinking she'd gone to any extra effort on his account.

The ready way she'd taken to life at the castle had her worried. After returning from her run on the beach, she had swum laps in the indoor pool, then soaked for half an hour in the adjacent hot tub. Her bones had turned to jelly, but she had felt almost indecently good.

Perhaps because her conscience was troubled by how much she'd enjoyed wallowing in so much luxury, she'd spent the rest of the day on her private terrace, working on her laptop. In the hot tub, an idea had come to her for Maxim's film, and she was anxious to capture it.

When told that Annegret preferred a working lunch in her suite, a servant had brought her a bowl of delicious crab consommé and crusty bread, and a selection of tropical fruits drizzled with orange liqueur. Yes, she would need to be careful or she'd start getting used to this level of attention.

Maxim's attention was another matter entirely, she thought, frowning as she tucked lip gloss into her black raffia purse. She'd been the one to suggest dinner tonight as the prize in their contest. Not the smartest move, if she didn't want to spend more time with him than she had to.

That she might be using Maxim to bolster the self-esteem that had taken a battering at Brett's hands, she had also considered while she was working. It was flattering to be pursued by a prince. And in Maxim's case, safe, since nothing could come of it.

So why did she feel as if she was making a mistake going out with him this evening?

She had her hand on the house phone, trying to summon the courage to call him and make some excuse, when there was a knock on the door. Expecting a servant, she opened the door to find Maxim standing outside.

Annegret would never know how tempted he had been to actually fly her to Noumea for dinner, Maxim thought as he approached her suite. What was the good of being royal if you couldn't indulge yourself now and again?

Unfortunately, he had long ago learned the folly of this kind of thinking after inviting a dozen school friends to play hide and seek in his father's palace at Taures while his parents were out. Seven-year-old Max had ordered the servants to produce snacks and soft drinks, and the afternoon had turned into a chaotic romp. It was a wonder the antique furnishings and priceless art collection had survived their shenanigans.

When Prince Gabriel found out, Maxim had been called before his father to account for himself. He still remembered shifting from foot to foot, feeling a slow burn travel up his neck and face, as his father reminded him that they lived in a palace only by the grace and favor of the Carramer people. What Maxim had used as playthings were held in trust for future generations. In return, the family were required to serve their people. Maxim must never think it was the other way around. Maxim had never again abused his position.

Not that he wasn't tempted. Noumea was a comfortable ride by long-range helicopter. He could ply Annegret with champagne and canapés en route. He smiled, picturing her pleasure at the ride and the treats. She might pretend to be blasé about staying at the castle, but he hadn't missed her enthusiasm over being waited on and pampered.

On her first day he'd amused himself by having a masseuse sent to her suite, although he was man enough to insist they dispatch a female. The very thought of another man in such intimate contact with her had made the prince bristle, although he had avoided examining the reason too closely.

In the guise of a casual inquiry, he had later learned that Miss West had thoroughly appreciated the gesture. For someone as doggedly opposed to royalty as she was supposed to be, she had taken to royal life remarkably well, he thought. Pulling out all the stops to fly her to another country for dinner would be a positive pleasure.

Except he wasn't seven years old anymore and he was well aware of the public furor that would ensue if he pulled such a stunt. And he'd have nobody to blame but himself. Even if he paid the cost out of his private income, he would be setting a pretty poor example.

Maxim sighed heavily. There were times when he wearied of doing the right thing. Never taking advantage of his position. Scrupulously keeping his feelings in check in case he ran afoul of the blasted Champagne Pact. What had his ancestor been thinking when he'd signed away not only his own right to love as he chose, but that of succeeding generations?

According to history, a wave of migration from Europe two centuries ago had threatened to overwhelm the province's resources. The royal family had needed the Soral dynasty's goodwill to help build more schools, hospitals and roads. At the time, signing away a little thing like love probably hadn't seemed too high a price. Today, Max wasn't so sure.

Why was he thinking of this now? he wondered. He was happy with his life. He believed passionately in the work he did for the Merrisand Trust. He had only to think of the thousands of children who had benefited to remind himself why he gave so much time and effort to the cause.

He had his hobbies, like his observatory where he could study the heavens—his other passion in life, though indulged far too infrequently through lack of time. He ran, he swam, he played tennis. And his social life wasn't exactly a desert.

Right now he wasn't planning on marrying anyone, so love didn't enter into the picture, did it? He could enjoy the company of a woman like Annegret without wanting more.

She didn't strike him as being in the marriage market, either. According to his sources, she was on the rebound from the man whose father was her boss. He must be an imbecile to think she wasn't good enough for his son. More likely it was the other way around.

Thinking of her running alongside him this morning, Maxim felt a smile tug at his mouth. Anyone who'd seen her flying along the sand like a vision would consider himself lucky to share the same planet with her. She was gorgeous.

More than that, she had backbone, unlike some of the vapid royal women Maxim was supposed to show an interest in. Maybe he was influenced by his sister, Giselle, who was very much her own woman, even to the extent of marrying the man Max had hired to run the royal deer park. Giselle wouldn't let anyone tell her what to do, although Max himself had tried often enough. As her older brother, he considered it his duty.

Their mother, Princess Marie, was also a strong woman, so he had plenty of examples to inspire him. A yes-woman wouldn't cut it. Nor would one of those giggly, simpering creatures his mother's society friends paraded before him from time to time.

The Champagne Pact had its uses, he thought, if it protected him from such creatures. Unless one of them happened to be royal. Then he would really be in trouble.

If Annegret had been royal…

She wasn't, so he was wasting his time thinking about it. They could be friends, but nothing more. It didn't stop him from wanting her, but there was nothing wrong with that. He may be prince of Taures, but he was still a man, and she was a beautiful, desirable woman. Nothing abnormal about imagining what she'd be like in his bed. Or even taking her there, for that matter, if she was willing.

Maybe that was the solution. Dinner first, slow dancing to soft music, then let the evening take its course. Get her out of his system.

He had a feeling it would take a lot more than one night.

When she opened the door in answer to his knock, he was sure of it. She looked as if she had been poured into her slinky black dress. When she moved, the amount of leg revealed by the slits at each side had him gulping for air. Maybe they could just forget dinner and move straight on to dessert.

"You look beautiful," he said, wondering if the strain he felt could be heard in his voice.

Evidently not. "Thank you," she said, sounding pleased. "So do you."

"Men don't look beautiful," he replied.

He did, Annegret thought. He was wearing a modern charcoal dinner suit, the longer jacket perfect for his height and broad shoulders. The collarless style framed his aristocratic features, and the whiteness of his dress shirt made his tan glow.

However good it looked, she wanted to see him without the suit, she thought, surprising herself. While acknowledging the sexual sparks flying between them, they had managed to behave civilly around one another. Even when she'd been running with him on the beach this morning, with neither of them wearing more than the essentials, she hadn't let her imagination run away with her.

It ran riot now.

She could picture him all too clearly stripping off the suit and the linen shirt. Carelessly throwing them aside. Then coming to her with blazing eyes, slowly sliding the sensuous fabric up over her hips, higher and higher, until he could whip it over her head and cast it aside. He would run his hands down her body, skimming over the narrow bands of lace that were the last things coming between them, before discarding them, too.

She became aware of her breathing quickening, and

made an effort to slow it—to slow the insane thoughts running through her head. It wasn't going to happen between them because she wasn't going to let it. She didn't intend to be seduced by him, knowing how it would have to end. That she might be halfway there already didn't bear thinking about.

"We aren't really going to Noumea, are we?" she asked, annoyed to hear how husky she sounded.

His dark gaze lingered on her face, as if his thoughts had been running along similar lines. Oh Lord, she hoped not.

"Would you like to?" he asked.

She felt her color rise until her mind belatedly sorted out what he was asking. "I spent a working holiday there once and loved it, but it's crazy to go so far for one night."

As if he couldn't stop himself, he brushed the side of her face with the back of his hand. "Haven't you ever felt like doing anything crazy?"

She felt that way now. But she tried for flippancy. "If I do, I lie down until the impulse passes."

"And if it doesn't?"

"Mostly it does, so I haven't had to answer that yet."

Moving like a sleepwalker, he stepped into the room and pulled the door shut behind him. She heard a click as he engaged the lock. The eager leap of her heart contradicted her logical mind warning her that she didn't want this. Didn't want to acknowledge what was between them, although it was as vibrant as another living presence in the room.

She'd told herself that as long as they ignored it, it would go away. It wasn't fair of Maxim to change the rules now. Why didn't he simply take her out to dinner—even to Noumea or the moon? She didn't care. They could discuss her ideas for his film, keep things on an even keel between them. Pretend nothing else was happening here.

Then he took her in his arms and it was impossible to pretend any longer. As he molded her against him, she released a sigh she recognized as surrender. She was right where she wanted to be, where she'd dreamed of being since the moment she'd set eyes on him.

To the hands she slid across his back, he felt as unyielding as she'd suspected. She explored him through the fabric of his suit, then grew impatient and slid her fingers under the jacket, moving around to his chest, where she flattened her palms over the sculpted outline of his pectoral muscles.

Lost in the wonder of the experience, she would have explored lower, but when she reached his belt, he caught hold of her hands and tugged them out of his jacket. Clamping them in his, he raised them to his lips, kissing her fingertips, then nibbling on them, the sensation of his teeth grazing her sensitive skin making her eyes widen.

She felt an answering pull deep inside her, and twisted, instinctively trying to escape the ferocity of her response. He wouldn't let her. His grip tightened and he used his other hand to press her closer, keeping her in place until her tremors subsided, the way he might have restrained a nervous colt until it became accustomed to his touch.

Her every sense felt magnified and focused, as if her entire world had spiraled into this one moment. She stilled her movements, although every instinct counseled escape. The why of it was as scary as it was exhilarating. She wasn't usually nervous in a man's arms. So it had to be this man making her so afraid.

She didn't fear anything he might do, she realized. More what she might do, giving him more of herself than she had ever given to any man, although Maxim hadn't asked anything of her.

But he would.

She wasn't usually given to premonitions, but she had one now. Of herself letting him make love to her, completing the fantasy she had started when she saw him on the threshold. She shuddered, seeing herself making him a gift of everything she was, then waiting in vain for anything in return.

The premonition shook her to her core. She didn't fear his touch, and definitely not his kiss. She craved them as a hungry person craves sustenance. What she feared was giving him everything and being left with nothing, as her mother had been.

Perhaps it should have, but the fear didn't stop Annegret from lifting her face to Maxim and parting her lips in breathless anticipation.

When he lowered his mouth to hers, the fear was swamped by more primal urges: to see his eyes bright with wanting her; taste the flickering of his tongue against her lips and teeth; inhale the masculine scent of him, while her ears were filled with the rasping of his breath, a ragged echo of her own.

Her overloaded senses reeled. She clung to him, glorying in the torrent of sensations pouring through her. The play of his mouth against hers was sweet torment, making her ache with wanting more. Wanting to be filled with his power and passion.

A primitive sound stirred between them, barely rec-

ognizable as the moan of desire she was unable to
hold back.

Had she ever truly been kissed before? She had
thought so, but nothing had prepared her for this. Her
knees started to buckle. He released her hand and
wrapped both arms around her, steadying her. Or both
of them. Opening her clouded eyes, she was amazed
to see him looking as shaken as she felt. Perhaps he
hadn't expected the kiss to get so far out of hand.

Or anticipated her effect on him.

She took some satisfaction in that. In the signs of
her power over him. It allayed a little of her unease.
Not nearly enough, but sufficient for her to murmur,
''Do you still think we shouldn't go too far for one
night?''

Maxim dragged long fingers through his hair, spik-
ing it. He was glad he'd locked the door because he
knew any servant coming in right now would spot his
aroused state at a glance. Bad enough that his pants
felt three sizes smaller than when he'd walked in here,
without him becoming an item on the servants' grapevine.

He'd thought he'd been the one kissing Annegret.
Getting her out of his system. If he hadn't felt so darn
uncomfortable, he would have found the idea laugh-
able now. Somewhere in midkiss she'd moved into
the driver's seat, hitting the accelerator until he was
hurtling along with her, as out of control as the rawest
teenager on his first date.

He was well aware that they'd nearly gone a lot
further than he'd intended. And he wasn't thinking of
a dinner date. In another few minutes, their destination would have been the carved four-poster in the

next room, although from there, they could have traveled to the stars.

Getting ready for their night out, he'd seriously considered it, to the extent of tucking a condom into his breast pocket, then another for luck. They were both single, both free to spend the night together if they wanted to. His body was still telling him how much he wanted her. So why hadn't he let it happen?

Annegret was the problem, he told himself. Despite her veneer of worldly wisdom, he recognized her vulnerability. She'd admitted being hurt recently. And there was the emotional baggage of her mother's experience with a prince's equerry. Maxim wasn't stupid enough to hold himself accountable for all the royal indiscretions in the world, but he didn't want to add to Annegret's burdens. Somehow he knew if he took her to bed, it wouldn't end there. And it had to if he was to retain his crown.

"We both know we've gone quite far enough," he said tautly.

He hadn't meant to sound accusing, but she heard it, anyway. "It was only a kiss. No big deal."

She didn't mean that, either, he saw, but let it stand. "I'm glad we agree." Every instinct urged him to remove the hurt shimmering in her eyes by kissing her again. He managed to take a step away instead. "Then all that remains to be decided is where we have dinner."

She crossed her arms over her chest, the gesture unconsciously defensive. "For some reason I'm not that hungry anymore."

He knew the reason, because he shared it. "All the same, you need to eat. I've had a table set up in the rose arbor, with a wonderful view of the lake. At short notice, it's the closest I could come to your fantasy destination. It's a perfect evening. We may as well enjoy it.''

She wouldn't enjoy it for the same reason he wouldn't, he understood, as a shadow of defiance darkened her lovely features. Maybe they should have gone to Noumea, after all. It would have been a lot less disturbing than where he had almost taken her.

He saw her wrap her self-possession around herself like a cloak. ''As you wish. You're the prince.''

He nodded, wondering if she had any idea how much he would give right now to be able to deny it.

Chapter Six

On the phone the following day, Annegret heard the concern in her mother's voice, "Are you sure that going on a cruise with the prince is a good idea, with the Champagne Pact standing between you?"

Annegret had asked herself the same thing ever since Maxim kissed her last night. Now she shared the only possible conclusion with her mother. "The pact isn't standing between us. The cruise is strictly business. I need interviews with the prince and his rival to have a fighting chance of convincing the network to renew the show next season. And I won't get the interviews unless I agree to make a documentary about the trust for the prince." Or so she'd told herself as she'd tossed and turned after her dinner with Maxim had ended.

Bad enough that she'd had to sit across from him in the most romantic of settings, eating a meal she'd barely tasted, and pretending nothing had happened between them. The worst of it was, he behaved as if nothing had. A kiss that had wrenched her to her soul seemed to have left him unscathed.

Royal reserve was an art form the prince would have learned from infancy, she'd told herself. Or he could have kissed an army of women and she hadn't even made the cut. How else could she explain his refusal to take things further? If he'd shown any sign of wanting to she knew she couldn't have denied him, even knowing the pact made anything lasting impossible. All she'd wanted was for the magical way he'd made her feel to go on and on.

Evidently she was the only one.

Preoccupied with her thoughts, she hadn't fallen asleep until almost dawn, and felt wretched now. Going out to sea with a group of strangers was the last thing she felt like doing. But anything else would signal to Maxim that his kiss had been a much bigger deal than she wanted him to know. And if they were to work together, she wasn't about to hand him that much power over her.

She realized that Debra was well into a mother-daughter lecture on the dangers of setting off alone with a man Annegret barely knew.

"There will be a hundred people on this cruise. I'm hardly likely to be alone with Maxim," she pointed out.

"So it's Maxim, is it?" her mother replied without missing a beat.

Exasperation made Annegret tighten her grip on the phone. Why hadn't she sent a postcard instead of calling? She asked herself the same thing every time they had this kind of conversation. And since she called home every few days from wherever she was, they invariably ended up having this kind of conversation.

Much as she loved her mother, sometimes they drove each other crazy. Too much alike, Debra said. Annegret wanted to deny it, but heard herself sounding like her mother often enough for it to be scary.

"The prince invited me to call him Maxim," she said. What would her mother say if Annegret added that he had kissed her senseless last night, leaving every nerve feeling raw?

Her voice must have betrayed her, anyway. "How long have you been in love with this man?" her mother asked.

Debra knew her too well to believe an outright denial. "All right, I *am* attracted to him. A lot. That doesn't mean I love him, or that there's anything to be done about it."

"Something can always be done."

"Not unless you know a way to rewrite history."

Silence from the other end of the line made her suspicious. "Mom, it was a figure of speech, not an invitation."

Laughter greeted the warning. "What a suspicious mind you have, Greta," her mother said affectionately, using her nickname for her daughter. "Of course your love life is your own affair. Just know that I love you and want you to be happy."

"I know." And she did know. Annegret wouldn't call so often otherwise.

"Tell me more about Maxim's rival, Chad Soral. I hear he's quite a ladies' man."

"He may well be, but I'll be too busy to notice him, too," Annegret said, trying not to clench her teeth.

"You're taking a television crew with you?"

"Not at this stage. I have a lot of research to do first."

"Then how can you be too tied up to notice two of the world's most eligible men, when they're going to be throwing themselves at your feet?"

Annegret restrained a sigh. One of them was most definitely not going to be throwing himself at any part of her. The other she had still to meet. "Maybe I should have a torrid shipboard romance with one or both of them. Can I tell them it was my mother's idea?"

"Don't take that tone with me. You may be a big shot TV producer, but I'm still your mother."

"Sorry, Mom," Annegret said, as much to forestall another lecture as because she felt truly contrite. One day it would dawn on Debra that Annegret was twenty-seven years old. It probably wouldn't make any difference. Annegret had a feeling Debra would still be giving motherly advice when she was seventy and her mom was ninety-five.

She wouldn't really mind, she discovered. For all the friction that occasionally surfaced between them, they were good friends. And Annegret appreciated the sacrifices her mother had made on her account, giving up her work in the diplomatic service to give her little girl a good start in life. It couldn't have been easy for Debra to set aside her own heartbreak and devote herself to raising her child.

Accepting that she was on her own, Debra had sold her apartment and used the proceeds as a down payment on a rundown boardinghouse on the Central Coast of New South Wales. While pregnant, she had redecorated it herself on a shoestring, turning it into a successful bed-and-breakfast that had provided for them both. Her mother's former diplomatic contacts had ensured a plentiful stream of visitors looking for somewhere pleasant and relaxing to stay.

For the first few years of her life, Annegret had been blissfully unaware of her mother's struggle. As a child, all she'd known was the freedom of the beach near at hand, and a supply of interesting people who spoiled her.

It wasn't until she was seven and had asked about her daddy for the umpteenth time that Debra had told her the story of her birth—omitting her father's name in case Annegret was tempted to go looking for him, she had figured out much later. At the time she hadn't understood what it had meant to Debra. Her mother had put such a positive spin on the outcome that Annegret had believed they were better off with just the two of them. Exactly as her mother had intended.

"I love you, Mom," she said on impulse now.

Her mother's laughter trilled across the phone lines. "And you think that will get you off the hook?"

"It always has before."

"And it will now. Just promise me you won't do anything foolish on this cruise."

"Define foolish," Annegret teased. "Are we talking falling overboard, overindulging at the buffet, what?"

"I mean the kind where you come home with your heart in little pieces," her mother said softly.

That hadn't happened since Annegret was a teenager. Her mother still didn't know the real reason why she and Brett had parted. At least Annegret hoped she didn't. Debra had done her best by them both. It wasn't her fault if it wasn't enough for the likes of Brett and his father.

"How are the LOLs?" she asked, changing the subject.

A couple of years ago her mother had sold the boardinghouse for a good price, buying herself a town house in a smart new development next to the beach, with enough money left to free her from the need to earn a living. She now volunteered at a home for frail, elderly women.

Going along to help out whenever she was between projects, Annegret had christened them the LOLs, for little old ladies, and the name had stuck. Lately the women had adopted the tag themselves as a badge of honor. Such a feisty and fascinating group were they that Annegret had been toying with the idea of telling their stories on film.

As she'd hoped, Debra regaled her with tales of the group's latest doings, forgetting all about Maxim.

"How's your own love life?" Annegret asked after a time.

"I'm fighting the men off, as usual," Debra said gaily.

It was more of an admission than Debra realized, Annegret thought. At first she had worried that she was the reason her mother wasn't involved with anyone, other than on the most casual basis. Gradually, she'd understood that Debra had given her heart to Annegret's father, leaving no room for any other man.

Annegret burned with dislike for her unknown parent. He didn't deserve Debra's devotion. But fair was fair. She didn't want her mother meddling in *her* affairs. She should show Debra the same courtesy. "As long as you're happy," she declared sincerely.

"More than you know," her mom said. She hesitated, then added, "This week I heard from some of my old friends in the diplomatic service that another revolution in Ehrenberg had led to the restoration of the monarchy.''

''On television this morning, I saw the news about the rightful king being restored to his throne,'' Annegret said. At the first mention of the European monarchy, her attention had been caught. Now she felt her heart sink. It was bad enough that her mother still mourned her lost love, but Annegret hated to see her torture herself, hoping for progress after all these years. By now the man probably didn't even remember Debra's name.

Feeling as if their roles had been reversed, Annegret said, ''Should you care, when you know nothing can come of it?'' Deliberately she repeated her mother's own words.

A beat, then, ''I'll always care.''

Yes, she would, Annegret knew as she said goodbye. She hung up, feeling angry on her mother's account and her own, if she was honest. First her father, then Brett, and now Maxim. Were she and her mother fated to be involved with wealthy, privileged men who had no compunction about tampering with their emotions?

Well, not anymore. Annegret might have fooled herself into believing Brett's empty promises, but she wasn't going to be seduced by Maxim's kiss. This time she knew the score. Strictly business, she reminded herself as she got ready to attend the launch.

The magnum of champagne felt cool in Maxim's firm grip. As prince of Taures, he had launched his share of vessels, but this one was special. The first journey of the *Princess of the Isles* wasn't to provide pleasure for the well-off, but to provide enjoyment and respite for people who needed it the most.

In his speech, he had conveyed his gratitude to the Soral Shipping Line and Chad Soral in particular, for placing the ship in the service of the Merrisand Trust. Chad's reply assured the prince and the onlookers that it was a privilege to help such a worthy cause.

Time to get on with it, Maxim thought. With the traditional words, "God bless her and all who sail in her," the prince swung the bottle. It crashed against the pristine white hull, showering the bow with champagne. The band struck up the Carramer national anthem, "From Sea to Stars," and the audience joined in enthusiastically.

Standing at attention for the anthem, Maxim surveyed the crowd from the podium. Official visitors mixed with locals and tourists, attracted by the fanfare. The most excited were the family groups who had been invited on this shakedown cruise. Every family had at least one ill or disadvantaged child, their young faces etched with signs of their struggle simply to survive. Today the struggles would be forgotten, for a few days anyway, as the families enjoyed themselves on the cruise.

As if drawn by a magnet, Maxim's gaze found Annegret among the members of the media. Not by a twitch of a muscle did he betray the instant physical response he felt at seeing her there, but he was surprised how much discipline it required. Last night he had kissed her, supposedly to get her out of his system. A lot of good that had done. He could still taste her on his lips and feel the eagerness of her supple body molded against him. It wasn't helped by catching sight of her in the crowd.

Whoever said that the best way to handle temptation was to yield to it didn't know what they were talking about. Kissing her had only made him want more.

Much more.

This morning she was dressed in a white pantsuit over a vivid cerise shirt, and she looked like a butterfly among her colleagues. She really was astonishingly beautiful. Earlier he had glimpsed her bags being carried on board the vessel, and had been startled by the pleasure stabbing him at the sight of the labels in her handwriting.

This would have to stop.

He started to tear his gaze away, but she looked up and caught him watching her. Her mouth widened in a revealing smile that vanished almost at once. The change gave him a totally unwarranted feeling of satisfaction. So he wasn't the only one affected by last night's encounter. He should probably feel badly at how close he had come to seducing her. Instead he felt a glow of anticipation, as if last night had been a prelude to something even better.

He had no business thinking of her in this way, much less contemplating acting on the thought. It didn't stop him from wanting to. Or from deciding that the prospect of spending the next three days on board *Princess of the Isles* suddenly seemed a lot more appealing.

Before that, there were official duties to be dealt with. He already knew most of the VIPs, so few introductions were needed. Nevertheless, after half an hour Maxim's jaw ached from smiling for the many cameras, both local and international. He seriously doubted whether much of what he said would make it on air, but duty demanded he say it, anyway.

He took far more pleasure in greeting the families who had been invited on the inaugural cruise. They seemed surprised when he asked for them to be presented to him, but soon lost their shyness when they saw he was genuinely interested in them. Before long, he had a pretty four-year-old girl called Sophie hoisted in one arm and her three-year-old twin brothers shadowing his every move.

"Looks like you've made some new friends," a husky voice said from close behind him.

He turned. Annegret had also been adopted by a small girl and a boy, brother and sister from the look of them. Maxim's heart clenched at the sight. She seemed so relaxed in the toddlers' company that they could easily have been her own children.

"Enjoying yourself?" he asked.

She brushed hair out of the little boy's eyes, the gesture so natural that a tight fist of longing gripped Maxim. "I've never seen so many happy, smiling faces in one place," she said.

She lowered her voice and spoke close to his ear. "You'd never know there was anything wrong with these kids, but their mother tells me they've spent more time in the hospital than at home. It seems so unfair."

The fierceness in her tone echoed his own sentiments. "That's where the trust comes in, ensuring they don't have to cope alone."

The prince's equerry drew him aside for a quiet word. The prince frowned, then lifted his shoulders in apology to his young friend. "I have to go and meet the captain and crew."

Sophie's arms tightened around his neck. "Can I come with you?"

The prince smiled at the little girl. "It's going to be boring. I'm sure you'd rather go with your family and see what your cabin looks like. That's your home on the ship," he explained.

The child's eyes grew round. "Are you coming on the ship, too?"

The prince hugged her. "You bet, so I'll see you again on board."

"Mama says there's a swimming pool. I can show you how good I can swim."

"I'll prepare to be impressed." He returned Sophie to her beaming mother. She distracted the children by pointing something out on the ship, allowing Maxim to slip away to do his duty.

The mother turned to Annegret. "Isn't the prince amazing? I never expected he'd talk to us, far less hold Sophie. He isn't at all what I expected royalty to be like."

She wasn't the only one, Annegret thought as she nodded in agreement. For all the research she'd done into various royals for her show, she hadn't gotten close enough to any of them to understand what their lives were like. She was starting to see that being a prince wasn't all luxury and privilege. She didn't want to feel compassion for Maxim, but she could hardly help it. Along the wharf she could see the captain and senior officers of the *Princess of the Isles* being formally presented to him. Maxim had looked happier meeting the young family.

It wasn't hard to see why. They had to deal with daily struggles that most people couldn't begin to imagine. As part of her preliminary research, Annegret had read some of their stories and been moved to tears. There could be few tougher challenges than the possible loss of your child, yet they faced it with a courage that amazed and inspired her. Some even credited their difficulties with teaching them as valuable life lessons.

Would she be so courageous in their shoes? Hoping to have children of her own one day, she prayed she would never have to find out. In the meantime, she wanted to do what she could to honor their example. She was toying with the idea of telling the story of the Merrisand Trust through the eyes of the children who benefited most. She wasn't sure what Maxim would think of it, but if he wanted her expertise, he would have to let her do this her way.

"Look, they're handing out streamers."

The two children who had been clinging to her wrenched free and went to get some streamers to throw from aboard ship as she sailed. Annegret would have to go on board soon, but she felt oddly reluctant. On land, she felt sure she could resist Maxim's appeal. At sea, it might be another story.

Despite telling her mother that she would see little of the prince during the cruise, she wasn't sure it would work out that way. He was bound to want to discuss her plans for the film. Keeping things businesslike wasn't going to be so easy when just being around him set her nerves zinging.

Seeing him with the children hadn't helped. Her creative mind had immediately leaped to a vision of him surrounded by his own children—small, serious versions of himself. She would have to work hard to ensure they had the best of both worlds, her ordinary one as well as his royal one.

Now where had that thought come from? When had she jumped from keeping things strictly business to fantasizing about being the mother of his children? It was a natural response to seeing him with the families today, she thought. As a producer, she tried to think herself into a scene, see it through the participants' eyes. How else could she make the story come to life?

This wasn't about her and Maxim, she lectured herself as she made her way through the throng to where the passengers were filing onto the ship. She had filmed dozens of human interest stories while keeping her emotional distance. This was no different.

As she started up the gangway, she saw the prince being escorted along an upper deck, his bodyguards ranged around him. Of course it was different. None of the human interest stories she'd filmed before had involved a man like him. Even from a distance, he made her heart drum a disturbing tattoo. Her index finger had skimmed her lower lip in imitation of his kiss, before she realized what she was doing and let the hand drop.

Thoroughly alarmed, she spun on her heel. Nothing could happen if she didn't go on the cruise. She could send the prince a message that she was unwell, or had a phobia about sailing and realized at the last minute that she couldn't handle the voyage. There was a kernel of truth in both excuses.

She hadn't allowed for the passengers boarding behind her. Closest was a tall, good-looking man who grasped her arm and steadied her, stopping her from bumping into him. "Forgotten something?"

With a moment's reflection, Annegret realized her panic seemed foolish. She could handle this. She forced a smile. "I thought I had, but it's okay."

His sea-green eyes sparkled and his generous mouth widened into a grin of pleasure. "I'm delighted. I'd hate to sail without you, Miss West."

She had instantly recognized his finely chiseled features from the speeches and her research, but was surprised that he knew who she was. "How do you…?"

"When Maxim told me you were joining us, I made a point of finding out more about you. The photo on your company's Internet page doesn't do you justice. I'm Chad Soral."

Chapter Seven

By now she thought she had an answer to almost any line, but Chad's compliment had a disconcerting ring of sincerity. She settled for a simple, "Thank you, Mr. Soral."

"Chad, since we'll be working together. I hope I can call you Annegret."

Her pulse picked up speed. Was it really going to be this easy? "Sure, Chad. I'm looking forward to interviewing you."

Deliberately she made it sound like a fait accompli, and was pleased when he didn't contradict her. "As long as you're not planning to do it right here. We're holding up the wheels of progress."

As the owner of the shipping line that had built this vessel, he could hold things up if he liked, she thought. Her chance to escape the cruise had passed, so she continued moving toward the security people checking the credentials of those coming aboard. She couldn't help contrasting Chad's down-to-earth manner with the pomp and ceremony surrounding Maxim. Of course, Maxim was a prince and Chad a commoner, but the latter had earned his position.

Maxim had earned his, too, she thought in fairness. He may have inherited his title, but she had seen how hard he worked. He could have enjoyed a life of ease and comfort. Instead, he chose to put in long hours on behalf of children like those she'd just met.

When had she become the prince's cheering section? she wondered as she offered her papers for inspection. Chad was waved straight through, waiting for her beyond the gangway. Once on board, she was greeted by a receiving line of crew members, who straightened a fraction more when they saw who was with her.

Hearing the cabin number she was given, Chad frowned and said something Annegret didn't catch to one of the crew. The woman consulted a clipboard. "One moment, Miss West, I've given you the wrong number. You're in suite two on Pacific Deck. I'll have someone escort you."

"It's all right, I'll show Miss West the way," Chad said. "We're practically neighbors."

He led her through a garden atrium that would have done a five-star hotel proud. When her media credentials had been brought to her at the castle, they had included a map of the ship, so she knew that the atrium was the hub of the vessel. Restaurants, a café, outdoor pool, movie lounge, fully equipped fitness center and even an art gallery radiated from it. She hoped for the time to explore at least some of them.

"Why did you change my cabin allocation?" she asked as she followed Chad up a wide, sweeping staircase.

He looked unconcerned at being found out. "I have to look after the media."

Seeing some of her colleagues heading down to a lower deck, she thought his concern was fairly selective. But she wasn't complaining, especially when it became obvious that Pacific Deck was VIP country. At the far end of the corridor she saw a security man stationed outside another set of doors. Annoyed at the way her heart skipped a beat, she told herself it was nothing to her if Maxim also had a suite on this deck.

Chad paused beside a double door with a gold number on it and slipped a plastic card into a slot. The lock clicked and he swung the door open and handed her the card. "If you need anything, your steward will provide it. I've told the purser you're my guest."

This was news to her and possibly to Maxim. Unless the prince had made the arrangement with Chad in the first place. She would ask the prince about it at the first opportunity. "You shouldn't trouble yourself on my account."

The tycoon's sea-foam eyes lingered on her face. "I have a confession to make. I'm really softening you up. I have some idea of employing your professional skills to make a series of documentary films about the Soral Shipping Line."

Excitement edged up her spine. She had told Maxim she didn't do corporate work, but for an assignment on that scale, she'd happily reconsider. She narrowed her gaze as suspicion overtook pleasure. "The prince didn't put you up to this, did he?" She wouldn't put it past him to engineer a reason for her to remain in Carramer so she would agree to make his film for the trust.

Chad looked put out. "If anything, he tried to convince me you wouldn't be interested. I take it you *are* interested?"

Not sure if she was glad or sorry that Maxim wasn't behind this, she decided she'd be a fool to turn Chad down without finding out exactly what he had in mind. "I could be."

"I'm delighted to hear it. You're a beautiful woman, Annegret. I hope business won't be all we get to discuss during the cruise."

Her head felt light. Here was one of the world's most eligible bachelors telling her he wanted to see more of her. And not only because of her professional skills. "I'm flattered," she said sincerely. "But—"

He touched a finger to her lips, silencing her. "No buts. Join me for dinner tonight?"

Although tempted, she wavered. Chad was attractive, and he was obviously no shrinking violet. Nor was he known as a one-man woman. But she could see no harm in enjoying his company during the voyage. What with Brett's rejection and Maxim's lack of availability, she was ready for some uncomplicated flattery. "Thank you, I'd like that."

He gave a half bow. "I'll see you at eight in the main restaurant."

"I'll look forward to it."

She'd look forward to it a lot more if the date was with Maxim, she thought as the cabin door closed behind Chad. She felt a frown furrow her brow. A moment ago she'd been glad he wanted to distract her. Now she was unhappy because he wasn't the prince. Some people were never satisfied.

Annoyed with herself, she turned her attention to her accommodations. She was sure she was the only member of the media to qualify for a two-room suite complete with king-size bed, bathroom with whirlpool tub, a large bay window and balcony off the living room. If this was work, she could get to like it.

It *was* work, she reminded herself, pausing in her exploration. A lot of people's jobs hinged on getting her show renewed for another season. She had better straighten up and fly right, or sail right in this case, and make the most of this opportunity.

Chad Soral found her attractive enough to merit special treatment. She should not only be flattered, she should be working out how best to turn his interest in her into a blockbuster interview. Before she could think about the project he'd dangled in front of her, she had her show about the Champagne Pact to produce.

She was interrupted by a steward delivering her bags from whatever cabin she had originally been allocated. He refused a tip but cheerfully showed her how everything in the suite worked. Left alone again, she began to unpack, her thoughts busy.

Her task was almost done when another knock caught her attention. The same steward waited outside, his arms filled with red roses. Carrying them inside, the man could barely conceal his glee as she reached for the card taped to the vase.

"Welcome aboard. Join me for dinner tonight at eight." It was signed "M."

A sensation of pleasure so acute it was close to pain erupted through her. In spite of the demands on his time, Maxim wanted to have dinner with her. It was quickly followed by desolation. "Would you take a message to Prince Maxim's equerry?" she asked the steward. "Ask him to thank the prince for the flowers and pass along my regrets. Tell him unfortunately I already have a dinner engagement."

Strange how hard it was to say. Even harder to imagine dining with Chad, knowing that Maxim was bound to see them together in the restaurant. Why hadn't he asked her sooner? she thought furiously, as the steward left on his mission. She would far rather have dined with Maxim.

He probably wanted to talk business, but if so, why send red roses? In the language of flowers she understood they meant love, although maybe they had a different meaning in Carramer. Whatever it was, she didn't need it.

Her emotions felt tied up in knots. The prince had no right to send conflicting messages to her when they both knew how it must end. It was probably just as well she had accepted Chad's invitation before receiving Maxim's. She might have done something foolish. Like accepting. As it was, her decision was made.

Hearing a muffled announcement that they were about to sail, she decided to leave the unpacking and go out on her private balcony to watch. Hundreds of colored streamers already linked the ship to the shore. The band on the wharf played a medley of show tunes.

She leaned against the white railing. It was a perfect day. Both sea and sky were the same seamless azure, promising smooth sailing. Both her interview targets were on board and competing for the right to spend time with her. She wasn't only reporting this adventure, she was part of it. Why didn't she feel like the luckiest woman alive?

It was *because* the two men were on board, she told herself as the ship slid away from the wharf, the widening swathe of blue water the only sign that they were moving at all. One by one, the streamers snapped against the side of the vessel or drifted back to shore. With a few last waves and calls, those left behind moved away.

She turned back inside, haunted by the suspicion that she had agreed to have dinner with the wrong man.

Deliberately, she arrived late. Not late enough to be rude, but for the restaurant to be already bustling by the time she got there. With any luck Maxim would be busy with other people and wouldn't see her join Chad.

Luck was against her. Not only were she and Chad not dining alone, but she recognized many of the people seated at the prominently located round table as important benefactors of the Merrisand Trust. At least Maxim wasn't among them, she thought with a rush of relief, although three empty seats remained across the table.

Chad held out a chair for her and murmured, "You look stunning."

He wasn't so bad himself, in a dinner suit that looked as if it had been molded on him. Telling herself she was dressing to please herself, she had chosen to wear a sheath in softly draping black fabric threaded with silver. She had bought the dress in a boutique in Merrisand Village after learning about the cruise. She had been drawn to the uneven hemline, realizing only belatedly how much thigh it revealed on one side with every step she took. Chad didn't seem to mind. ''Thank you,'' she said as she took her place on his right.

She was mesmerized by the three vacancies, wondering who would fill them. A few minutes later she had her answer when the captain arrived, escorting Maxim and a dark-haired woman Annegret didn't recognize.

She wasn't jealous, she told herself. No reason to be. But seeing how easily the prince had replaced her as his dinner guest, she couldn't help feeling miffed. With the rest of the diners, she stood as the captain, the prince and his companion took their seats.

The table was too large for introductions to be made across it, so she was left to wonder at the woman's identity as Chad introduced the table companions closest to them. Automatically filing the names and faces in her mind, Annegret made the right responses, but she felt preoccupied. Not that she cared who the woman was, she told herself. If Maxim was lucky, she had royal blood and could solve his romantic problems for him.

Still, for the first time in her life, Annegret knew how it felt to want to physically attack another woman. Amazed at her thinking, she took a sip of water, but the cooling drink had little effect on her heated blood. The closer the two heads across the table got, the more she wanted to do bodily harm.

Determinedly, she began chatting to Chad, wondering if she wanted to show Maxim or herself that she wasn't troubled in the least by her replacement.

As she toyed with an appetizer of delicately smoked coral trout, she became aware that Chad had asked her a question she hadn't even heard. ''I'm sorry,'' she said with a disarming smile.

Chad glanced across the table to where Maxim and the dark-haired woman were deep in conversation. "I asked if you'd met Baroness Montravel."

Annegret frowned, not liking the idea of her rival being titled, not that she was competing. Hadn't she speculated about that very thing only moments ago? "Why do I feel as if I should know the name?" she asked.

"Her husband is Mathiaz, Baron Montravel of Valmont Province. Apart from being a tireless worker on behalf of the Merrisand Trust, she's also probably the only female member of the royal family with a black belt in martial arts."

Annegret masked a quick flare of alarm. "Is royal life that dangerous these days?"

Chad shook his head. "For a time it was, at least in Mathiaz's case. He was being stalked by a disgruntled employee who turned out to have criminal connections. Mathiaz got in the way of a bomb, temporarily losing part of his memory." He indicated the beautiful woman. "Jacinta was his bodyguard at the time, and her quick action saved him from far worse injury."

Part of Annegret was cheering. Maxim and the woman were cousins by marriage. The word ricocheted around in Annegret's head: *marriage.* Her competition was married. She dragged her thoughts off the pointless merry-go-round. What difference did it make to her?

Resting her chin on her hand in a deliberately carefree pose, she asked, "Did the baron marry her out of gratitude?"

"Out of love. Unbeknown to anyone but Jacinta, they had fallen in love during the time he couldn't remember. While she was helping him recover, he fell in love with her all over again. It was obviously meant to be.''

Again Annegret had to work to stop her gaze from flickering to Maxim. "I don't believe in love being fated.''

Chad's hand closed over hers. "Pity. I became a believer as soon as I saw you coming aboard.''

She was glad they were served with their next course just then, saving her from the need to answer and letting her gracefully remove her hand from Chad's. Something in his tone rang hollow, as if he were playing a game with her. She was convinced that he hadn't fallen in love with her and had no intention of doing so.

So what *was* he doing? This time she did glance at the prince, but his attention was focused on the captain. She thought of her research. Chad and Maxim were not only rivals for the crown of Taures, but in other ways, as well. Like two stallions in the same herd, they had competed academically and in sports since their student days.

Knowing she was Maxim's guest, did Chad hope to use her to make the prince jealous? If so, it wasn't going to work. To feel jealous, Maxim first had to care about her, and he couldn't afford to. Physical attraction didn't count, and in any case, Chad couldn't possibly know about that astonishing kiss. Or that remembering it now made her feel dizzy.

As if picking up her thoughts, Maxim looked over and caught her watching him. Chad chose that second to take her hand again, and she could have sworn she saw the prince's gaze harden. Was she right? Was Chad hoping to score points off the prince? She withdrew her hand but it was too late. Maxim had already turned away.

What he thought was of no consequence to her, she told herself. Whatever Chad's motives, he was clearly interested in her. At least he was free to pursue it. Why shouldn't she enjoy his attention while it lasted?

But he was using her, and more importantly, he wasn't Maxim. The thought slammed through her like an arrow to the heart. However eligible and attractive Chad was, and she had to grant he was an impressive man, he didn't send her heart into overdrive the way the prince did so effortlessly. Oh Lord, she wasn't falling in love with Maxim, was she?

The notion sent a shiver through her. Chad gave her a look of concern. "You're not unwell, I hope?"

Not in the way he meant. "Fortunately, I'm a good sailor, and this vessel is as steady as a rock," she said.

He nodded as if she'd paid him a compliment. "That's how the Soral Line builds them. You're bound to be aware of some movement, but you'll soon get your sea legs."

So gentle had been the ship's progress that she had hardly been aware of it, but she nodded, letting Chad think it was the reason for her reaction. It would also give her an excuse to retire early, if it came to that.

"I'd like to give you the grand tour tomorrow," he continued. "What time would suit you?"

"Anytime you're free," she agreed, trying not to wish the suggestion had come from Maxim. It was time she stopped acting like a lovesick puppy and started doing her job.

"Shall we say ten, then? I'll meet you at the steps leading to the bridge."

"Is it all right if I bring a camera? I usually take a few instant photos so I can put together a story-board."

He inclined his head in agreement. "If you wish, I'll have the ship's photographer take them for you."

"The Polaroids will be fine. They're only for my own reference," she said, not wanting to be any more in his debt than she needed to be.

His eyes shone with approval. "I'd rather it was just the two of us, too. After the tour we can discuss your project in intimate detail."

At his choice of words, ice filled her veins. She liked Chad and was grateful for the help he seemed more than willing to provide. But intimacy wasn't what she wanted from him. "It will take me a little time to get my thoughts together before I'll have anything to discuss," she said.

He made an expansive gesture. "I'm at your disposal whenever you're ready."

"You're being more helpful than I've a right to expect."

He let his gaze linger on her face, his fingers playing a soft tattoo against her arm. "I'm not always this comfortable with someone from the media. Burned too often, I imagine. But you're different, Annegret. I knew it the moment you bumped into me coming aboard."

"Don't, please," she said. She might be cutting her own throat, but she couldn't let him think the attraction was mutual when it wasn't. "I'm here to do a job, nothing more."

"For now, anyway," he said, sounding undeterred. "Just remember what they say about all work and no play."

Relieved, she nodded. "I'll remember."

Somehow she finished the meal, thankful that politeness demanded she pay attention to the elderly man on her left. He turned out to be a famous Carramer pianist who gave concerts in aid of the Merrisand Trust. He was scheduled to play during the cruise, she learned, pleased when her tentative suggestion that he might contribute to the sound track for her program was received with enthusiasm. The pieces were falling into place, she decided. If only she could keep her recalcitrant emotions in line.

Declining Chad's invitation to join him at a concert being given to welcome the passengers, she wasn't entirely pretending when she gave the ship's motion as her reason. She wasn't seasick exactly, but neither did she feel particularly well. She also declined his offer to walk her to her suite. "I know the way. There's no need to spoil your evening."

"Without you, it's already in ruins," he said, but his eyes danced, letting her know he was teasing her. When she looked back, it was to find him deep in conversation with the attractive blonde who'd been seated on his left at dinner.

So much for undying love.

Was she crazy, resisting such an attractive man who obviously found her appealing? Annegret asked herself as she made her way toward her suite. Maybe she was just plain hard to please.

On impulse she turned and headed for the door leading to a recreational area at the bow of the ship. Reserved for the handful of Pacific Deck residents, the area was shadowy and deserted now, the lounges and quietly bubbling hot tub empty. She didn't mind. With most passengers at the concert or other evening entertainments, she was happy to have the place to herself.

Leaning against the railing, she filled her lungs with the salty air. Above her, the sky was a dark blue velvet canopy studded with more stars than she had known existed. It was impossibly romantic, but also a reminder of her barren love life. Why couldn't she make herself want the man she *could* have, instead of the one she couldn't?

Unfortunately, it wasn't that easy.

A sound made her spin around. Maxim stood watching her, one shoulder angled against the bulkhead. Light and shadow played across his features, sharpening them. Accustomed as she was to seeing him surrounded by his security people, it took her a moment to realize that he was alone. Since it could only be by his choice, she wondered at the reason.

Hearing her catch her breath, he asked, ''Waiting for someone?''

The answer was out before she could stop herself. ''Yes. You.''

Chapter Eight

She could hardly believe she had said something so revealing. It wasn't as if she'd meant it. Make light of it, pretend it's a joke, she urged herself, heart thumping. "Of course, I say that to all the men in my life," she added before he could draw a breath.

With the menacing grace of a cougar, Maxim prowled toward her, stopping close enough for the scent of his cologne to envelop her. The bittersweet aura spoke of forest leaves newly crushed underfoot, of citrus and sandalwood, and Maxim's own brand of maleness. She couldn't help it. She drank him in with every shallow breath.

"Men like Chad Soral?" he asked.

Her heart gave an awkward skip. Surely the prince wasn't jealous? "Chad isn't *in* my life," she pointed out with scrupulous honesty. She wished she had the strength to move away. When Maxim stood this close, she could hardly think straight.

His eyes sparked with fire. "I got a different impression at dinner tonight. You spent a lot of time holding hands.''

So Maxim hadn't been as distracted by his baroness as Annegret had thought. No reason for her spirits to leap. It only meant he'd noticed everything around him, as usual. ''Chad's the kind of man who likes to touch. Some men just do,'' she stated.

''Depends on how much temptation is put in their way.''

One thing was certain—her friendliness toward his rival had left the prince far from happy. What that meant, she hardly dared explore. ''Are you accusing me of leading Chad on?'' she demanded, not sure if she was irritated at the suggestion or with herself for lacking the courage to walk away, leaving the prince to stew in his own suspicions.

His jaw tightened. ''It's Chad I'm worried about.''

Anger bubbled inside her. ''So you followed me to warn me not to take advantage of my position here?'' Such a thing had never occurred to her, and her temper steamed at the implied criticism. She might consider herself lucky that Chad was making her job easy, but she had never thought of seducing him to get what she wanted. She didn't work that way, and it was time Maxim learned that.

He gestured at the luxurious facilities around them. ''It didn't take you long to get yourself moved from the lower deck.''

''It was Chad's idea, not mine.'' She folded her arms defiantly. ''With all due respect, I don't see that it's any of your concern, Your Highness.''

''This ship is sailing under royal patronage, on behalf of the Merrisand Trust. Everything that goes on aboard it is my concern.''

Some of her pride deflated like a pricked balloon. He was only worried about the effect on the trust if a scandal blew up over Chad and a member of the media. Annegret drew herself together. "Thank you for your concern, but it's misplaced. I'm not planning on sleeping with Chad, or any other man aboard." To ensure Maxim got the message, she spat the words out with machine-gun precision. "If you're finished lecturing me, it's late and I'm tired." None of which was true. It wasn't that late and she'd survived far more demanding days, at least physically. Emotionally, today was right up there.

Before she could slip past him to the sanctuary of her suite, the prince caught her arm and whirled her around to face him. "I didn't think you would try to seduce Chad, but that he might take advantage of you. I've known him most of my life, and he's never been inhibited around women. Nor is he troubled about the trail of broken hearts he leaves behind."

A little of her anger dissipated, but not much. Her scorching look should have reduced Maxim's hand on her arm to ashes. Instead, she was aware of a throbbing sensation deep inside her, competing with the anger. "And you think I can't handle that?"

"You shouldn't have to." He dragged his fingers through his hair. "I'm trying to warn you, Annegret. Chad doesn't mean to be, but he's a predator. He's so used to getting his own way that he doesn't see the damage he's doing. You deserve better."

"I'm not a little girl," she said softly, feeling the last of her anger leach away. She tried to cling to the shreds of it as a defense, but it was too late. The prince was working his magic, and in the moonlight, under the brilliant canopy of stars, she was a sitting duck.

"Believe me, I know that, too." His tone sounded ragged, as if she wasn't the only one feeling the power of the moment.

"Then why don't you let me deal with Chad in my own way?"

"Because I've been through this before." Maxim took a steadying breath and she wondered what kind of battle he was fighting with himself. She soon found out. "When we were at university, there was a woman I really cared about. I suspected she felt the same about me."

I don't want to hear this, Annegret thought. It was obvious there had been no happily ever after, but everything in her rejected the thought of Maxim loving another woman. "Chad went after her?" she anticipated.

Maxim nodded. "He knew the Champagne Pact stopped me from doing a damn thing about it. I had to step back and watch him steal her heart."

It occurred to her that a heart so easily stolen might not have been his in the first place, but nothing would be gained by saying so. "Why didn't you fight for her?"

"What was the point? I had nothing to offer her."

Annegret almost swooned in his grasp. Had Maxim looked in a mirror lately? Even without a crown, he had more to offer a woman than any man she had ever met. "You underestimate yourself," she said. "You don't have to be a prince to win a woman's heart."

"In Chad's case it was the truth," he said, bitterness shading his tone. "He had social position, money to burn and no historical straitjacket holding him back.''

''Does your history have to be as much of a strait-jacket as you're letting it be?''

Flames lit his dark gaze. ''How can it not? If I follow my heart, I become the last de Marigny to wear the crown of Taures. How would you like that written in your epitaph?''

Tempted to ask where his heart would lead him if he allowed it, she clamped down on the question, afraid she might not like the answer. ''I guess I wouldn't. But there are courts of law. Wills can be challenged. Why not a provision like the Champagne Pact?'' On whose account was she asking? Maxim's or her own?

''Do you think I haven't had lawyers sifting through the documents, looking for loopholes? The pact was conceived by some of the most devious minds in the land—Chad's forebears. They designed it so it couldn't be overturned, only allowed to run its course. In another twenty-five years, my son—assuming I find a sufficiently royal mother to bear one—will be free to do as he pleases.''

Everything in her rejected the notion of Maxim married and a father. Not the married or father part. Only the idea of someone else making them possible.

Glad he couldn't see her expression in the velvety darkness, she closed her eyes against the anguish rocking through her. When had she started to care so much about his future? When it became entangled with hers? He was spelling out all the reasons why that wasn't going to happen, yet part of her refused to accept it.

The stupid part, she thought angrily. Quite possibly

the part she had inherited from her mother, who had made the same mistake, loving a man who had other priorities. Maxim wasn't for her. Get it through your head, Annegret ordered herself. Getting it through the rest of her was far more difficult, especially when her body insisted on responding so vibrantly to his touch.

His hand was still on her arm, no longer holding her in place, but linking them together lightly, as if he didn't know he was doing it. She knew, though, as quakes of desire shook her.

She fought to ignore them. "Can't your cousin, Prince Lorne, make a law decreeing the pact null and void?"

Maxim gave a hollow laugh. "Lorne rules Carramer but my family controls Taures Province. Under Carramer's constitution, Lorne can't overrule provincial laws except where national security is involved, and this hardly qualifies. Besides, Lorne is a great respecter of the law. When his first marriage turned out to have been made in hell, he refused to change the law to legalize divorce in Carramer. If his first wife hadn't died, I'm sure he would have gone on suffering for a lifetime rather than change the law to suit himself. He believes no member of the royal family is above the law, not even the monarch."

And certainly not the prince of Taures, she understood. She knew he wouldn't welcome her pity, but her heart wanted to melt for him. So much for her long-held assumption that royals had the world handed to them on a silver plate. His plate was laden with burdens she had never suspected.

How must it feel to grow up knowing your destiny from day one? Not for Maxim the freedom to dream grand dreams and wonder if they might come true.

She knew he loved the stars. Might he have yearned to be an astronomer? Or hoped to travel to other planets himself one day? Launching ships and sending emissaries in quest of their dreams was the closest he was likely to come. He didn't even have the right to choose whom he loved.

"Have you ever been tempted just to walk away from it all?" she asked softly.

"Sometimes."

"And yet you don't. Why not?"

"For the same reason a general doesn't abandon his troops. He's their leader. In return for their fealty, he owes them the best leadership he can provide."

"At least a general chooses his profession."

"True, but having chosen it he loses part of his freedom."

"You could always hand the crown over to Chad. He seems capable of handling the job."

"And he has no constitutional impediment to loving as he wills."

The sudden sharpness of Maxim's tone ripped at her. "I'm only thinking of you," she assured him.

"You aren't suggesting I should abandon my crown so your new friend can inherit it?"

Really angry with him, she tried to move away, but his other hand clamped around the railing, so she was imprisoned in the circle. With his body against hers and his mouth only a breath away, she was swamped by the longing to touch and taste.

It made no sense. He thought her the kind of woman who directed her affection wherever it benefited her the most. A growl of fury caught in her throat. What had given him the mad idea that she not only wanted Chad, but wanted to rule Taures at his side? That Maxim believed her capable of such a thing showed how little he understood her.

She might make her living in a fantasy world, but that was no reason to move in and live there. That was how her mother had condemned herself to a lifetime of futile hopes and dreams. Annegret was the last person to want to repeat the mistake.

"Have you finished?" she said, letting her quiet tone convey how angry she was with him.

"Hitting a little too close to home, am I?" he demanded.

She brought her chin up. "You might be, if I was as mercenary as you seem to think. Whatever makes you think I *want* a crown, yours or any other man's?"

She'd surprised him, she saw from the momentary confusion reflected in his gaze. His frown deepened. "Isn't it what every woman wants?"

Was it wishful thinking, or did he sound a tad less sure of himself? Maybe the prince had only known women who were attracted to him because of his position. He needed to know that she wasn't among them. "I can't speak for every woman, only for myself, but after my mother's experience with a man from royal circles, a crown is the last thing I want."

"So if I proposed marriage to you right this minute, you'd turn me down?"

"You could always try it and see."

Whatever had possessed her to issue such a challenge? A very strange feeling took hold in the pit of her stomach at the idea of Maxim proposing to her. She didn't want him to, of course, but what if he did?

He couldn't, she assured herself. Not without risking everything. It didn't subdue the wondering, or the sharp sensation of desire accompanying it.

For several heartbeats he simply looked at her, before saying slowly, "I've never been more tempted by an offer in my life."

A huge lump lodged high in her throat. She swallowed to clear it. "Then it's just as well the Champagne Pact forbids it, because I'm not interested, either. A royal lifestyle is the last thing I want for myself."

Taking his time, he grazed her cheek with the back of his hand. "Aren't you even a little curious about how we'd be together?"

"N-no."

Her attempt at certainty sounded woeful even to her own ears. Yet she'd meant what she said about not repeating her mother's mistake. End of story. But curious about him as a lover? Could she honestly tell herself she wasn't?

There was nothing intrinsically wrong with letting him make love to her. They were both adults, both unattached. As long as she expected nothing else from him. And that's where things got complicated. Maxim's kiss had already shown her that if she allowed anything more to happen between them, she would end up getting hurt.

Coward, she chided herself silently. She had left Chad alone at the table because he wasn't Maxim. Now she was ready to run and hide from Maxim because she might get hurt. If she kept this up, she was in for a long, lonely spinsterhood.

Perhaps the prospect was what made her turn her cheek into the prince's hand, nuzzling into the warmth and comfort that was there for the taking. He didn't move, but she heard him suck in his breath as she rubbed her face back and forth. It was as if another woman had inhabited her body when she experimentally drew lazy circles on his palm with her tongue.

"Dear heaven, Annegret."

His ragged response reminded her she wasn't the only one making this decision. He had some say in it, too. That she might have ignited a fuse she couldn't easily extinguish also occurred to her. Strangely, the thought was not as troubling as it should have been. "Just indulging my curiosity, as you suggested," she said, her voice low and smoky with desire.

He might be a prince, but he was also a man and he had his limits, Maxim thought. Right now he felt pushed to the very brink. He also felt confused. Seeing Annegret holding hands with Chad during dinner, he had wondered what she was up to.

It wouldn't be the first time a woman had tried to play the two men off against each other. Not that it was much of a contest. Thanks to the Champagne Pact, Chad invariably got the girl. Except for that first time at university, Maxim hadn't really cared. This time he did.

Strangely enough, he believed Annegret when she said she wasn't interested in a royal marriage. Her mother's experience with her father was enough to make anyone gun-shy around royalty. But Maxim hated to be judged by another man's shortcomings. He would never have left a woman he loved alone and pregnant with his child. No matter what it cost him, he would have found a way to be with her.

He wanted Annegret to understand that about him.

The flick of her tongue against his palm had him sucking in his breath. Much more of this and his hormones would be making decisions for both of them. He grabbed her hand and brought it to his lips, letting his teeth worry her fingertips.

It was her turn to catch her breath. Good. He wasn't the only one in deep here. He slid a hand around her nape, letting his fingers tangle in her hair. The strands feathered against his palm.

With his other hand he pulled her closer, giving in to his rampaging need to feel her body against him. Her perfume clouded his senses, or maybe it was the sheer female essence of her drugging him, making him ache with a thousand needs and desires.

They were in a public place. Someone could interrupt them. He didn't care. For perhaps the first time in his adult life, he couldn't make himself heed the risk of discovery or scandal. More man than prince tonight, he only cared about filling himself with the heady sensations the woman in his arms brought to him.

He heard her whisper his name, sounding breathless. Her hands splayed across his chest, skimming over his thundering heart. Then she thrust her fingers into his hair, pulling his head down. He couldn't see her expression in the shadows, but when her mouth found his, there was no mistaking the fire in her. Did she feel the same sense of sharp, aching pleasure? The need that was like flames leaping inside him? Her kiss fanned the blaze higher, giving him all the answer he needed.

For her sake he should fight the fire. Deny himself everything she offered and that he so much wanted to give her. Yet he couldn't stop himself from touching her, tasting her. Every tremor of her response made him shake with need.

Annegret had sensed they would come to this. Had it been like this for her mother? The wanting, the craving eclipsing all common sense? Annegret finally began to understand why her mother had succumbed, and had gone on loving so hopelessly for so long. Some things were beyond choice.

When Maxim lifted his mouth from hers, she couldn't hold back a cry of protest. He steadied his hands on her shoulders, not letting her closer but not letting her move away, either. Just keeping her there while their breathing slowed and the seascape slipped back into focus.

"Why?" she asked when she could control her voice.

"You know why."

"You don't have to stop. Whatever you have to give will be enough."

She could see that her words moved him perhaps more than her kisses. He skimmed a finger over her top lip, eliciting a shudder. "For now, perhaps. Maybe for a long time. But what about when I have to marry someone else?"

After the poetry of his touch, the blunt reminder hit her like a shower of cold water. But she understood his reasoning. If she couldn't deal with the spoken truth, how could she handle the future reality? "I didn't know it could be like this," she admitted shakily.

His hands cupped her face. "It's a revelation to me, too. You're a gift I never thought I'd receive. And it hurts like hell knowing I can't have you."

The pain in his voice flayed her spirit. She should be glad he was being strong for both of them. Instead she felt irate. She was a capable, modern woman whose family history, if not her own experience, had taught her not to expect a happily ever after. She could deal with this, take whatever he offered and be content.

But he was the one stepping out of the shadows into the light, drawing her with him and saying a decisive good-night. The magic had passed. He had turned into the prince again, she saw when the light spilled across his face. She almost expected to see his bodyguards turn up to form a protective cordon around him, but it was only her imagination. The only barrier between them was his damnable royal reserve.

She had been right all along. Princes were trouble, she told herself as she left him to return to her cabin. She was better off without the involvement.

The first thing she noticed when she went inside was the dizzying fragrance of his red roses.

Chapter Nine

"The ship is built on the submerged twin-hull principle called SWATH, which stands for 'small waterplane area twin hull,'" Chad informed her. "The engines are in the hulls beneath the waterline to cut down noise and vibration, and there are stabilizer fins on the front and back of each submerged hull to reduce motion."

From the bridge she could glimpse the very tip of the deck where Maxim had kissed her last night, she discovered.

"And down there is where the crew sets up the plank they make people walk who daydream on the tour."

"What?" She wrenched her attention back to Chad. After a restless night she couldn't entirely blame on the unfamiliar surroundings, she'd been in no mood for a guided tour of the ship this morning, but here she was. Unfortunately, only physically so far. Just as well her miniature recorder had captured everything he'd said. She clicked it off and tucked it into her shoulder bag beside the instant camera she'd used to take photographs for her storyboard. "I'm sorry, my mind was wandering," she apologized.

He gave her a rueful look. "Too bad it isn't in my direction. Although it's probably my own fault. Ship-building is so much in my blood that I forget everybody doesn't share my passion for the nuts and bolts."

"Then you won't make me walk the plank?"

"Only if you refuse to spend the rest of the day with me."

She hesitated. "I really do need some time alone, to think." It wasn't stretching the truth too far, although she had more on her mind than film projects.

"Take all the time you need. I meant it when I said I hope you'll agree to work for the Soral Shipping Line."

"If the alternative is being made to walk the plank, I'd better say yes. I'm terrified of sharks."

He hooked an arm through hers. "You strike me as a woman who wouldn't be afraid of anything."

Being alone too much, never knowing love, or never having a child of her own. She had a feeling Chad didn't mean those kind of fears. "I could give you a whole list," she said.

He escorted her off the bridge. "I hope you will. I'd like to get to know you better, Annegret."

Her laugh was uneasy. "In the interests of working together?"

"Naturally." But his hand tightened possessively on her arm.

Maxim had a hard time not clenching his teeth at the sight of Annegret leaving the bridge arm in arm with Chad as the prince and his party approached it. Her pencil-slim navy skirt was hardly the most practical garment for climbing around a ship, even one as luxuriously appointed as this. But he had to admit it made her legs seem longer and slimmer than ever. She had teamed it with a navy-and-white horizontal-striped top with a wide boat-shaped neck that left one shoulder bare. No sign of a bra strap, Maxim noted irritably. Hadn't he warned her about the kind of man Chad was?

Obviously it hadn't done the slightest good. Her eyes looked diamond-bright, and her generous mouth, emphasized by coral lipstick, was set in a wide, inviting smile that made Maxim want to step between them and ask her if she made a habit of playing with fire. He managed not to, but it took an effort.

Absorbed in her discussion with the other man, she headed off in the opposite direction without seeing the prince's party approach.

He had no reason to care what she did or with whom, he reminded himself. If letting her know what she was getting into with the shipping magnate wasn't enough, Maxim couldn't do much more.

He wanted to, he found to his chagrin. Right now it was all he could do not to haul Chad onto the deck and have it out with him, man to man. Teach him once and for all to keep his hands off...whom? The prince could hardly claim Annegret was his woman. He had kissed her twice, both times soaring to heights beyond his wildest fantasies. But kisses weren't binding. Annegret and he had an informal agreement to work together on her TV show and a film for the trust, but that didn't prevent her from spending her free time with any man she wished.

"Whatever you have to give will be enough," she'd said last night. If he'd had any sense, he'd have accepted the deal. Taken her to his suite and made love to her the way he'd dreamed of doing since he first set eyes on her. So what if he couldn't offer her marriage? She'd made it clear that she wouldn't marry royalty under any circumstances.

What had stopped him from carrying her to bed and sharing with her all he knew of pleasure? He could have learned from her, too, he didn't doubt. Last night she'd demonstrated that she had ample skills of her own to bring to their union. He felt his loins stirring at the very thought.

Annegret herself was the problem. She might think she was willing to settle for an affair with him, but he had seen her reaction when he spoke of the Champagne Pact. She might not want a royal marriage, but she *did* want marriage. The forever kind that meant you'd have children together, watch them grow up and have children of their own, while your hair slowly silvered and you learned to read your partner's thoughts.

Wanting the same thing himself, it wasn't hard to understand, although the restrictions on his love life meant he'd be lucky to find such a match. No matter how tempted he was—and heaven knew, she tempted him more than any woman he'd ever met—he wasn't going to deprive Annegret of her chance, in order to satisfy his own selfish desires.

Liberated, career-driven though she thought herself, he'd still seen the yearning she couldn't quite hide. Perhaps it came from growing up in a single-parent household, not knowing her father. Or from something within Annegret herself. But it was there, and she deserved to reach for her dream.

So it was just as well that Chad was showing an interest in her, since he could offer her what Maxim couldn't. The prince might want to kill him for it now, but in time he'd be glad she'd made the logical choice.

Probably about the same time the seas around Carramer turned into dust.

Annoyed with himself, he swung his attention back to the captain, who was proudly showing him the ship. Maxim interjected what he hoped were sensible questions, although only half his mind was on the answers. Why did he need to know how the ship ran? He didn't want to drive the blessed thing. It was enough that he could see the trust beneficiaries having the time of their young lives.

"I'd like to see the playrooms," he said on sudden impulse.

If the captain was surprised, he was wise enough not to show it. "Of course, Your Highness. This way."

Two decks down, after inspecting the nursery and a room full of computerized games for the older children, he was shown into a spacious glassed-in room. The window wall gave a sweeping view across the stern of the ship, but the small occupants were too caught up in their game to care about the stunning view. Shrieking with laughter, they ran, climbed and burrowed through a colorful obstacle course, under the watchful eyes of parents and staff. Only a closer look revealed that many of the children wore scarves over bald heads, leg braces, shunts taped into veins and other signs of their struggle to survive.

"Looks like they're having a good time, sir," the captain observed.

"That's the idea of this cruise. Most of these children have spent too much of their lives in medical care. They need some time away from those surroundings, where they can simply be children."

Noticing the prince, the adults started to their feet, but he waved them down. "Aren't you Sophie's mother?" he asked a startled woman who had begun to rise.

Reddening, she nodded. "Yes, Your Highness."

His gaze swept the room. "Where is she now? I don't see her with the other children."

The woman's eyes misted over. "Her father took her down to the ship's hospital. She's terribly seasick, poor thing. I came to check on my other children before I go there myself."

"I'll make a point of calling in on her shortly."

The woman's gratitude was palpable. "Oh, Prince Maxim, she'd love it. She hasn't stopped talking about you since you spoke to her on the wharf yesterday."

"The feeling was mutual. She's a lovely little girl." As pretty and vivacious as the daughter Maxim hoped he'd father one day, although without the health problems, God willing. He turned to the captain. "I don't want to keep you from your duties any longer, Captain. Thank you for a most informative tour."

The uniformed man snapped to attention. "My pleasure, Your Highness. I'm at your disposal anytime."

At Maxim's nod, the captain left. "No need for you to trail around after me, either," the prince told his two bodyguards. "Unless we're boarded by pirates, I'm safe enough while we're at sea."

They looked unhappy at the obvious dismissal. The senior one said, "As you wish, sir."

I do, thought Maxim, breathing a sigh of relief as they left him alone. He turned to the woman. "If you'd kindly show me the way to the ship's hospital, we can visit your daughter together."

Flushing with excitement, she bobbed a curtsy. "I'd be delighted, Your Highness."

As patron of several hospitals, Maxim had visited his share of wards, and the one aboard ship looked no different from those on shore. Newer and smelling of fresh paint, and with ocean views from every port-hole, perhaps, but still oppressive, to his way of thinking. It wasn't hard to find Sophie. She was the only patient and looked terribly small and vulnerable in the adult-size bed.

When she saw him, her pinched white face lit up. "Prince Maxim, you came to visit me."

He affected a stern expression. "What's this? Lying in bed when there's a playroom full of children missing you?"

"Daddy and the doctor said I had to be here. I don't want to be, honest," she said in a small voice.

"Then you're trying really hard to get well?"

The child nodded earnestly. "As hard as I can."

He smiled broadly and perched on the side of the bed. "Good enough for me. I've made a royal decree that all little girls aboard this ship have to spend half of every day playing. You won't let me down?"

Her tiny hand crept into his and stayed there, giving

him an odd sensation in the pit of his stomach. "I won't," she promised. "You're funny, like my daddy. Do you have any little girls?"

The odd sensation increased. "Not yet. Maybe one day."

"Can I come and play with your little girl when you do?"

"Sophie."

At her father's shocked tone, Maxim smiled reassuringly. "I have a better idea. After we get back to Merrisand, I'll send a car for you and your family and you can visit me at the castle."

The child's eyes grew round as saucers. "At the castle? Wow. Can I bring my dog, Pepper?"

Maxim nodded. "As long as he's castle-trained."

Sophie giggled. He was pleased to see that her color was improving. He stepped out of earshot long enough to gain the doctor's assurance that the child was only seasick, her leukemia still in remission. Then he returned to her parents. "I meant what I said about the castle visit. Make sure my equerry has your details and we'll set it up after the cruise."

Dodging their effusive thanks, he turned. And froze, feeling as if a giant hand was squeezing his heart. How long had Annegret been standing in the infirmary? With her gamine hairstyle, ridiculously short skirt and off-the-shoulder top, she looked almost French, reminding him of the women from Carramer's capital, Solano.

Her only concession to being aboard ship was her low-heeled leather shoes, which made her seem more petite than usual. He ached to take her in his arms, and thanked years of royal training for keeping the need from showing. "Hello, Annegret. I didn't know the ship's hospital was on your itinerary."

She shook her head, her hair fluttering coquettishly, making his heart squeeze even tighter. "It isn't. One of the other children told me Sophie was sick. I wanted to see how she's doing. Is she…?"

"Only seasick," he said quickly, hearing his own concern reflected in her voice. "I checked with the doctor. She's just keeping the child here as a precaution, so you can stop worrying that it's anything worse."

Annegret's body language telegraphed her relief. "Is it that obvious?"

"I felt the same way. Children like Sophie have a way of getting under your skin."

Not under Chad's, she thought. When she had expressed her wish to visit the hospital, he'd refused point-blank. "Can't stand the place. Any kind of sickness makes me feel really off," he'd told her.

"Yet you gave the trust the use of this ship to benefit sick children."

He'd spread his hands. "In business you have to do these things."

Her apprehension had increased. It was the kind of thing Brett and his father would say. "Good for public relations," she'd observed.

His gaze had cleared and he'd smiled. "I should have known you'd understand. You work in television."

Despite the tropical warmth, she'd felt a wintry chill. "Where people use one another all the time, right?"

Tightening his grip on her arm, he'd nodded. "Exactly. It's good to be with someone who understands the real world, especially when she looks as beautiful as you.''

That was when she'd realized her mistake. She didn't want to spend any more time in Chad's company. It wasn't going to make the longing for Maxim go away, only heighten it.

The moment she'd walked into the hospital and seen the prince at Sophie's bedside, talking so easily with the child's family, she knew she had made the right decision. Trying to fill the void inside her with another man's company wasn't going to work. Only one man could do that, and it wasn't an option. What that meant for her future, she hated to think.

Tension in every line of his body, Maxim looked over her shoulder. ''Isn't Chad with you?''

''I left him at the restaurant. He doesn't like hospitals.''

Maxim's mobile mouth eased into a smile. ''I should have remembered. When we were teenagers, we competed at everything. One day during a mountain bicycling race, I took a tumble and broke my ankle. If it hadn't been for my bodyguards, I'd still be lying on the mountain. Chad couldn't get away fast enough.''

''Remind me never to get injured around him.''

Her being injured at all was something Maxim didn't want to imagine. ''Some people just don't like the sight of blood. Chad has his own strengths,'' he said as charitably as he could. ''Are you going back to lunch with him now?''

''No,'' she said, glad her decision was already made. ''After this morning's tour, I have a couple of hours of tapes to transcribe.''

''For the trust or for your TV show?''

"Both," she informed him. "For the show, I want to concentrate on the Champagne Pact. The cruises really won't come into it. But they'll provide wonderful background footage for your documentary on the work of the trust."

Don't do it, don't invite her to join you. "I haven't eaten yet. Would you like to make it a working lunch?"

"I'd like that."

Her flushed coloring and the delight he heard in her voice told him he should have listened to himself. His own heart was beating too fast, the pounding of the blood in his ears drowning out common sense. "I'll arrange to have it served on the terrace off my stateroom, where we won't be disturbed." The last thing he wanted was for Chad to offer to join them. The memory of the other man's hand on her arm was too disturbing. It wouldn't do for the prince to deck his rival in a public dining room.

Dining alone with her isn't smart, either. Call it a working lunch, but at least be honest with yourself. You want her seated across the table from you, your hand on top of hers, seeing that soulful gaze directed only at you.

No he didn't. He wanted her in his arms with no table between them. And he wanted a lot more than his hand on top of her. Before the thought could get any more detailed, he dismissed it and gestured toward the exit. "After you."

Their cabins were on the same deck. He was careful not to touch her as they walked back, sensing that his royal control hung by a thread.

Lounging in the suite, his bodyguards sprang to attention as soon as the prince entered the spacious living area. The two men's expressions didn't change when they saw Annegret; they were too well trained. All the same, Maxim didn't want spectators. "Go and get something to eat. I'll be staying here for the next couple of hours."

With deferential salutes and murmurs of agreement, they departed. That left only the servants, and Maxim couldn't very well dismiss them if he wanted lunch, although he was tempted. He wasn't hungry, but Annegret probably was. She wasn't one of those women who ate like a sparrow, but goodness knew where she put the food. It didn't add an ounce to her slender figure. Maybe she had the same hollow legs his parents accused his sister of having.

Giselle's healthy appetite was one of the many things he appreciated about his sister. Her passion— for life as well as for her job as Keeper of Merrisand Castle—was another. She and Annegret were kindred spirits. Both had voracious appetites for work and for the rest of life's pleasures.

Who did he think he was kidding? Annegret might share many of Giselle's admirable qualities, but he didn't want to think of her in the same breath as a sister. He probably should, but it was beyond him.

"Make yourself at home while I organize lunch," he said, his husky tone more betraying than he wanted it to be.

Annegret didn't react. Depositing her shoulder bag on a low table, she curled up on one of the leather-covered banquettes and gave her attention to the ocean view from the window. "There's no hurry. I had a huge breakfast, so I'm not terribly hungry."

"Obviously you're not troubled by seasickness. The dining room was half-empty this morning."

"I noticed, although the sea feels like glass to me. I felt almost guilty digging into my sausage and eggs."

"Me, too." He couldn't help it; he leaned over and kissed her. It was a chaste, almost brotherly kiss, brushing her slightly parted lips before he straightened again. But the effect cut through him like a lightning bolt.

His throat muscles all but closed. "I won't be long."

When he'd gone, Annegret released the breath she'd been holding. She must be crazy agreeing to have a private lunch with him in his suite. Playing with fire had nothing on this kind of rashness.

Yet she knew she couldn't have refused if her life depended on it. Her fingers wandered to her mouth, where his kiss had left her lips tingling. She knew she was dangerously close to falling in love with Maxim, and she hadn't the faintest idea what to do about it.

If he'd been any other man, she could have had a passionate fling with him, gotten him out of her system and that would be that. This time it wasn't so simple. Not only was he the prince, but he touched her as she had never expected to be touched.

Not only physically, she realized, but in other ways that were more disturbing. Their shared concern for Sophie, for one thing. And how easy he was to talk to, as if there wasn't a social gulf a mile wide between them. If not for this other…*thing* complicating everything, they could be the best of friends, she thought.

Seeing him with the little girl in the hospital had given her the oddest feeling. It was as if she was viewing a different side of him yet again. She'd seen plenty of the royal prince, and far more of the man than was good for her. Now she'd glimpsed what he'd be like as a family man. The sight was breathtaking.

"Now what's on your mind?" he demanded, coming back into the room and seeing her worried expression.

She didn't mean to tell him, but emotional tension made the words spill out. "I was thinking about you and children."

Chapter 10

Pity help him, so was he, Maxim thought. Around Annegret, he found it hard to think about much else, "hard" being the way she tended to make him. Thinking of the beautiful children they could have made together, and how enjoyable that would be, was enough to set his blood afire.

"Would you care to be more specific?" he suggested, striving to keep his voice level.

She blinked as if emerging from a trance. "Forgive me, I didn't mean to speak so personally, Your Highness," she said quickly. "I've been toying with an idea of how we could film an update on the Merrisand Trust. Seeing you with Sophie today convinced me that the idea could work."

Believe it, she willed, clenching her hands together. Maxim as a father *had* been on her mind, but not in any way professionally. Her interest had been as personal as it sounded. Still was. If there had been any chance of a future with him…

There wasn't, she reminded herself angrily. The pact made any such prospect impossible. The reminder didn't make it any easier to pretend that her sole focus was on business.

His mouth narrowed. So they were back to "Your Highness" again. Maybe he was reading too much into her response to him. Right now she seemed focused on her work. "I see," he said, schooling his tone to a cool formality he didn't feel. "I look forward to hearing more about this idea. Right now we should move out to the terrace where our lunch is about to be served."

Food was the last thing on his mind, but he had to get her out of the suite before he did something reckless like kiss her again, this time with the unrestrained passion he could feel boiling inside him. Just as well the servants were hovering, he thought. In their presence he had to behave with royal decorum. How little of it he'd shown since meeting Annegret, he didn't like to recall. That would definitely have to change.

The prince's suite was located near the bow, and the terrace took up most of the forward deck. Screened from the view of the other decks by lush cane palms planted in deep troughs, the area was shaded by a white sail overhead, with artificial grass underfoot. A glass-topped table and two chairs had been set up to take full advantage of the ocean view. Crested glasses and silverware gleamed in the sunlight.

Maxim drew out a chair for her, doing his best not to touch her as she sat down. Since he badly wanted to, the effort made his tone sharp. "Did you enjoy your tour of the ship with Chad this morning?"

A servant unfolded a linen napkin across Annegret's lap and poured water into her glass. She waited till the man stood back before saying, "It was fascinating."

"I'm pleased to hear it."

The prince didn't sound pleased, she noted, feeling increasingly like an actor reading lines rather than saying what she thought. Probably because what she thought was too perilous to voice. She'd come close with her comment about him and children, but recovered sufficiently that she didn't think he'd guessed what had really been on her mind.

As the servant lingered, Maxim asked her, "Would you like some wine?"

With her thoughts already chaotic, she couldn't risk it. "No, thank you. I'll need a clear head if I'm going to get anything useful done today."

With a gesture he dismissed the servant, and then the prince turned his attention back to her. "You are entitled to relax and enjoy the cruise."

She leaned forward, toying with the silverware. "I am enjoying it. Chad was a wonderful host and guide."

"I saw the two of you leaving the bridge as I was going up to inspect it. You seemed to have a lot to talk about."

His cool tone suggested he had seen Chad arm in arm with her and didn't like it. Well, the prince was in no position to object, she thought. As long as she was off-limits to him, he couldn't dictate how she spent her time—or with whom.

Maybe that was the solution. Pretend there was something between herself and Chad. It would be a boon to her self-respect, and it would also make the point to Maxim that she didn't expect anything from him that he wasn't in a position to give her.

She couldn't do it.

"I like Chad, and he wants me to work for the Soral Shipping Line, so it's just as well we hit it off," she explained.

"Do you intend to work for him?"

Her finger drew circles on the glass tabletop. "I'm thinking about it. With my television show to consider, I won't have any free time until I get the next season in the can. And I've already agreed to work on your film for the trust, but I can do the development work for that at the same time as we're filming the Champagne Pact story. So I hope Chad isn't in any hurry."

"Chad is always in a hurry," Maxim said dryly. "As the controller of the Soral empire, he's not accustomed to being kept waiting."

"This time he has no choice. I'm not available," she said, putting a wealth of meaning into the statement.

An appetizer of succulent fresh seafood and salad was served, giving her a chance to compose her thoughts while they ate. She must have been mad to think she could be alone with Maxim and keep her mind on business. Every breath he took heightened her awareness of him as a sensual man.

Not a prince. A man in whose arms she felt more aroused than she ever had in her life. Last night he had made her forget why she hated anything to do with royalty. Had she actually told him she was willing to accept whatever he was able to give her? How quickly she had forgotten the bitter lesson learned from her mother's experience.

Maxim had made her forget.

Their plates were efficiently removed and he leaned closer. "Tell me more about your ideas for me—and children."

She set her glass down hastily. Concentrate, she ordered herself. Television production was a fast, furious profession. Normally she could multitask with the best of them. Why was it suddenly so hard to focus on answering a simple question?

Breathe, just breathe. "While touring the ship, I heard some of the children talking to their families, but especially to each other. They're so matter-of-fact about their problems that it would break your heart. I heard one little boy who couldn't be more than five or six telling his friend that he'd already made his will."

Her voice caught and she dragged in a lungful of air. Reaching across the table, Maxim tightened his fingers around hers, silently supporting her. His thumb brushed the base of hers. She clung to his hand while she got her breathing in order, then made her fingers relax in his, a task bordering on the impossible. "How do you stand it, and do the work you do, without breaking?"

"Somebody has to," he said simply. "The children have the best medical help in Carramer. They have their families for emotional reinforcement. As head of the trust, I'm supposed to clear the way and enable the parents and doctors to do their jobs. I can't let things get to me and still do my job effectively."

But he wanted to, she saw. As a prince he might be used to keeping his emotions in check, but they were there under the surface. She'd seen the sheen in his eyes, blinked away as fast as it arose. Had heard the compassion when he spoke with the children aboard the ship. The iron prince was no more than skin deep.

"It isn't all tragedy," he went on briskly, although she heard a slight catch in his voice. "The trust provides scholarships and travel opportunities for promising students whose families can't afford them, as well as recreational facilities in communities for children throughout the province."

While shopping for clothes for the cruise, she'd dropped in on a youth center in Merrisand, and she'd read about similar places the trust funded in other provinces. "I know. It's wonderful work. That's why I want to tell the story of the trust through the eyes of the children you help."

Finding the strength to pull her hand away, she saw his jaw tighten. He didn't like that. Well, neither did she, but they both knew why it was necessary. If she left her fingers tangled with his for much longer, they wouldn't have stopped at holding hands. He knew that, too. She saw the awareness in the shadowy way he looked at her.

"Go on," he said, sounding as if they were only discussing the film.

She tried to emulate his businesslike manner. "Sophie is such an articulate little girl, and so appealing. Not movie star pretty, but real. I want to use her as the narrator, introducing the other children as they tell their stories. The only adults we'll see will be through their eyes."

"It's a departure from the usual documentary style."

"That's why I like it." He was so cool that uncertainty gnawed at her. She wanted his enthusiasm. His approval. "Don't you?"

He steepled his hands on the table in front of him, silent for several minutes. "I think it's brilliant."

The breath whooshed out of her. She liked that he'd thought about her proposal and hadn't just snapped out an opinion. It made his endorsement all the more valuable. "Thank you."

"It won't be easy finding the right children," he added. "I agree that Sophie's a natural. Her parents strike me as the kind who would make your job easy. They're good people. Despite her problems, they don't let her get her own way in everything."

Annegret had seen that, too. "But if she genuinely wants to do this, they'll back her to the hilt. So all we have to do is find more children like her."

He waited until the servants had placed their main course of cheese soufflé in front of them, then said, "How soon can you start work?"

She had imagined that a cruise would be all sun and fun, but after her conversation with Maxim, the next twenty-four hours passed in a blur. Most of it was spent on the balcony of her suite making notes, roughing out a treatment for her scriptwriter to flesh out later, and putting together a rudimentary storyboard. She was no artist, but her stick figures showed what she wanted.

She should have concentrated on her TV show about the Champagne Pact, but instead found herself totally involved in Maxim's documentary about the Merrisand Trust. She had never known a project to unfold so fast.

Within a day of having lunch with him she knew

how she wanted his film to look. It wasn't going to be cheap. She assumed he would want quality work. If the budget was too high, she could reduce the number of location shoots, rearrange a few scenes, but that was grunt work. Amid the detritus of cold coffee and half-eaten meals she hadn't allowed the cabin staff to clear away for fear of breaking her train of thought, the film came to life in her mind. Now all she had to do was make it.

A knock on her cabin door heralded the stewards again, wanting to restore order, she assumed. It was probably time she let them. She got stiffly to her feet and went to answer the door.

Maxim stood there. She had been so steeped in her work that she wondered if she was still on the balcony, lost in thought. He dispelled the fantasy by stepping inside and pulling the cabin door shut. "What the devil do you think you're doing?"

He sounded so angry that she took a step back. "Working? Why?"

"For twenty-four hours straight?"

"I often do when inspiration strikes. I thought that's what you wanted."

He pulled her closer. "I don't want you to kill yourself with overwork. When you didn't appear for a couple of meals, I thought you might be with Chad, but this morning he said he hadn't seen you since yesterday."

The prince's voice sounded ragged. With worry over her, she realized in dismay. His tone suggested he hadn't liked the thought of her being with his rival, but hadn't come looking for her until he knew she was alone.

Her tongue darted out to moisten dry lips. She

heard him pull in a sharp breath. "I didn't think," she said simply.

His eyes blazed. "You didn't think I'd worry about you?"

She was too tired to choose her words. "I didn't think you'd care."

"You must know I care about you, Annegret. A lot more than I should."

She knew that, too. "I'm really sorry. But when I get caught up…"

His gaze went past her to the balcony. Through his eyes she saw the litter of crumpled papers, coffee cups and plates. Most of what was useful was safely in her laptop computer, but she still preferred to do most of her creative thinking on paper, and she hadn't yet mastered the art of storyboarding on a computer. "I made a bit of a mess," she said.

"Understatement of the year. Your cabin crew think I brought a madwoman on board."

"Is that what they call me?"

"Much more politely, of course. They think you're a writer. They're actually quite impressed."

She tried to think despite the confusion of sensations aroused by his hold on her. "I am basically a writer, but the end product comes out on film instead of between hard covers."

"Show me."

It was said in a tone of royal command. Habit, she decided. But she saw the fascination in his gaze as she led the way to the balcony and talked him through the rudimentary storyboard. "We close with Sophie planning her future, so the audience knows without us telling them that she's going to have one, thanks to the support of the trust," she concluded.

Maxim shook his head, making her worry that she'd disappointed him. "I can't believe you've done so much in a matter of hours."

But do you like it? she longed to ask. Not wanting him to know how much she cared what he thought, she waited in tense silence.

He planted a kiss on her forehead. "I already suspected that you're a genius. This leaves me in no doubt. Congratulations."

"Then you like it?" Good grief, why did she have to sound so needy?

"Of course I like it. Did you think I wouldn't?" He lifted her to her feet, his mouth finding hers in a proper kiss this time.

"I didn't know what to think." She was too exhausted to pretend indifference. Her emotions hovered so close to the surface that she couldn't help pouring them into her kiss. It should have left her breathless, but instead made her feel as energized as if she'd slept the hours away instead of working around the clock.

Belatedly, she became aware of her unkempt appearance. She was wearing the same faded jeans and soft white crossover top she'd changed into as soon as she returned to her suite after lunch yesterday. Her feet were bare, her shoes missing in action beneath the table.

Apart from washing her face and cleaning her teeth this morning, she hadn't given her looks a thought until now. She struggled to escape from his hold. "I must look like something the cat dragged in, if princes have cats."

"I believe Merrisand Castle has a number, but I don't see the connection."

She gave a self-conscious swipe at the hair falling across her eyes. "If you'd ever seen a mouse after a cat's been toying with it,, you'd know exactly what I mean."

He held her at arm's length, his expression enigmatic. "Why not try seeing yourself reflected in my eyes, rather than your mirror? I guarantee it's a far more accurate, not to mention entrancing, image."

Not sure how to convince her, he held on to her and gave her a minute to see herself as he was seeing her. Tousled as if from bed, with her face and feet bare, she looked utterly beautiful and desirable.

He saw the moment she believed him. Her smile only added to the stunning effect, and a tight fist of longing closed around his heart. It was hard to know what had felt worse, thinking she'd been with Chad, or finding out that the other man hadn't seen her. Both had sent Maxim into a frenzy of imagining.

Now, holding her at arm's length and staring into her glorious forget-me-not eyes, he knew he was dangerously close to falling in love with her.

Mentally cursing the Soral family and the hideous legacy they'd wished on him, he made himself release her. "Now that I know you're all right, I should get back to my duties." If he didn't, he wouldn't be answerable for the consequences.

Her pleasure vanished as quickly as the sun going behind a cloud, piercing him to the heart. "I should shower and change. Pack, too. What time are you leaving the ship?"

When she'd left his stateroom yesterday, they'd agreed that she would accompany him when the helicopter arrived to ferry him back to the castle later today. Knowing that Chad would be on board for the entire voyage, Maxim hadn't tried very hard to talk her into remaining. Now he wondered if he was being fair to her.

"You can still change your mind and stay," he offered. "You obviously didn't get much rest last night. A few more days of cruising might do you good."

"So you're saying I do look like something the cat dragged in?"

He was tempted to kiss her, but knew he would want much more. He made himself straighten. "This cat of yours can deliver you to me looking this good anytime. Trust me, you look beautiful. The helicopter will be here at six."

"Then I'd better let you get back to doing your prince thing," she said, sounding so diffident that he wanted to take her in his arms again. He didn't dare.

"Of all the ways I've heard my role described, this is the first time it's been called a 'prince thing,'" he said wryly.

Her smile gained strength. "Is that a capital offense?"

Keeping his face grave, he nodded. "Quite possibly."

"Then it's just as well I have the prince's favor."

Too sure of the likely outcome if he kissed her again, he lifted her hand and brushed his lips over the back of it. Intended as a courtly gesture, it left him feeling aroused and frustrated as the touch of skin to skin and the faint perfume clinging to her hand clouded his senses. She clearly had no idea how much of the prince's favor she'd already attained, and he left her alone before he could make the mistake of telling her.

Chapter Eleven

Since he had returned from the cruise, two days of trying to focus on work—doing his prince thing, as Annegret had called it—hadn't dulled Maxim's feeling of frustration. He knew if he allowed himself, he could fall in love with her. He was more than halfway there already. And more than halfway inclined to mount a legal challenge to the Champagne Pact that would shake Taures to its foundations.

The document itself was watertight. Generations of legal minds had proved it. But like an unfair will, it could conceivably be overturned if a modern court decreed it to be an unreasonable impost by the dead on the living.

What was it if not that?

To do so he would have to drag the royal family through a welter of legal proceedings that could undermine the stability of the province. His feelings for Annegret would come under the spotlight. She could well be blamed for the debacle. He couldn't do it to her or his family. Nor could he step aside in favor of Chad for the same reasons.

Sorely tempted, he slammed the folder shut. How was he supposed to concentrate on figures and reports when the only figure he kept seeing in his mind was Annegret's?

"Temper, temper."

He gave the intruder a searing look, then made an effort to relax as his sister took a seat beside his desk. He massaged his temples, where he could feel a headache starting. "You're looking beautiful this morning."

Giselle made a face. "Only this morning?"

"I'm your brother. My job is to keep you on the straight and narrow. It's Bryce's job to massage your ego."

At the mention of her husband's name, Giselle's eyes glowed. "A job he does magnificently."

While Maxim was officiating on the cruise, Giselle had been visiting their father and mother in Taures. "How was your weekend with the parents?" he asked.

"Since I married Bryce, they've been easier to deal with somehow. I think having Amanda around weakens their defenses."

Amanda was Bryce's daughter by his first wife, who'd died tragically after a long illness. "She is a charmer," Maxim agreed. On the eve of her fourteenth birthday, Amanda was already showing the promise of beauty, and for one not born to royal life, she had taken to it easily. Maxim already knew that their father, Prince Gabriel, the governor of Taures, liked being a grandfather to the child and wasn't shy about pressing Giselle to give him more.

"Amanda could soften any heart," he agreed. "Her behavior is regal enough to satisfy our mother's high standards."

Giselle laughed. "I'm glad one of us does. I'll never be the princess she wants me to be."

"I'm sure she's happy with you just as you are."

"Speaking of princesses—" Giselle leaned forward, lowering her voice "—I don't want to spoil the surprise, but I think you should know that they've picked out a princess for you. Talay Rasada of Sapphan, niece of the ruler, King Philippe. She's reputed to be a real beauty."

Royal circles were small enough that he knew of the princess, although they hadn't met. "And when do I meet this bride my parents have chosen for me?"

The coldness in his voice wasn't lost on his sister. "They're talking of inviting her to Carramer in the summer."

"They haven't yet done so?"

"Give them some credit, Max. They intend to consult you first."

Thankful for small mercies, Maxim reached for the telephone. "I shall tell them I'm not interested."

"Not even curious?"

"I won't have my life arranged for me."

Giselle stood up, touching his shoulder. "Whatever you decide, you know you have my unconditional support." At the door, she turned back. "You must love her very much."

He shot his sister a startled look. "Who?"

"Whoever makes it impossible for you to consider a future with Princess Talay."

"How do you know there's a woman?" However discreet he had tried to be with Annegret, servants gossiped. He should have known the efficient castle grapevine would have reached Giselle.

Her smile of understanding warmed him. "I didn't until your reaction confirmed it. Don't worry, your secret is safe. After everything I risked to marry Bryce, I know what love demands from you. But I also know how many blessings it confers in return. Only you know if the trade-off is worth it." Not waiting for a response, she left him to ponder her words.

There was plenty to ponder. Princess Talay's uncle, King Philippe, was an absolute monarch, and although his people were happy and prosperous, Sapphan was far less liberal than Carramer. Talay was likely to be the very model of a royal bride. But she wasn't Annegret West.

He couldn't imagine any woman, however beautiful, well-born or eligible, possessing Annegret's fire and passion. When something snagged her imagination, she was almost as single-minded as Maxim himself. She'd thought nothing of working all night on the cruise. Or leaving Chad Soral cooling his heels while she made sure a sick little girl was all right.

Maxim felt his mouth soften. He was guiltily pleased that she'd rejected Chad, although he wasn't sure she was acting in her own best interests. Chad could put the world at her feet. A world of money, power and privilege with none of the crushing responsibilities that went with being royal.

Noting his clenched fists, Maxim made himself relax. If he really cared about Annegret, he would be shoving her toward Chad instead of being glad she'd rejected the man. Why was his blood boiling at the very idea?

It was time he faced facts. As Giselle had suspected, he wasn't halfway in love. He was all the way, head-over-heels, in as deep as a man could possibly get. Princess Talay could never be enough for him, because Annegret already possessed his heart. The trouble was, she didn't want it, any more than she wanted a royal lifestyle. And he couldn't have her without giving up his crown, failing the people who depended on him.

If he had any sense, he would let his parents arrange the royal match, and do his duty as his forebears had done for centuries. Legendary love affairs had grown from less promising beginnings. His parents' marriage was a shining example. His mother, Marie, was the daughter of an ancient European royal house and had been betrothed to Prince Gabriel before their first meeting. From all accounts, the couple had been virtual strangers when they embarked on their life together. Yet his parents' union had endured for thirty-two years, their love growing and deepening with time.

A dull ache gripped Maxim as he considered the possibility for himself. Perhaps it would have satisfied him before he met Annegret. As silver would impress one who had never encountered pure gold.

She was pure gold. How could he settle for less?

How could he not, without forfeiting a kingdom? Slowly he took his hand away from the telephone.

Annegret finished typing the last of her notes into her laptop and closed the computer. She should feel pleased with herself. She had arranged a date and time when her TV crew could interview Chad Soral for the Champagne Pact story. She had been pointedly businesslike, making sure he didn't read anything into the arrangement. His response had been friendly, but tinged with an unmistakable air of regret.

She understood the feeling. It would have been easier if she had been attracted to Chad. He may well have been playing the field, as Maxim had warned her, but she could have handled that. More easily than the tumult of emotions the prince made her feel.

Before the cruise, Debra had asked Annegret how long she'd been in love with Maxim. How had her mother known before Annegret herself? She wished she could talk to her mother, but this morning her call had been answered by Debra's voice mail, and she hadn't called back yet.

Not that Annegret had let herself brood. With the crucial interviews lined up and her preliminary research into the Champagne Pact complete, she had turned her attention to developing the Merrisand Trust project.

Inspired by Maxim's enthusiasm, she'd had little trouble fleshing out her rough notes and sketches. Now all she needed was his approval of her plan and proposed budget, and she could start work in earnest.

No, that wasn't all she needed from him, she thought, standing up and pressing both hands into the small of her back. What she really needed she was never, ever going to get. Research had shown her what was involved if he married a woman not of royal blood. It wasn't just a case of changing places with Chad, but of ending his family's hereditary rule of Taures, disinheriting all future generations of de Marignys. Maxim would probably rather not marry at all, and have his sister's children succeed him, than go down in history as the last of the Marigny princes.

Not that the loss of his crown would change Annegret's feelings for him. Her own family history meant she could love him more readily as a commoner than as a prince. The very thought of his lifestyle made her shudder. How did he stand the constant demands of duty and having people watching him every waking moment? Growing up in a boardinghouse, Annegret had also been surrounded by people, but she had been able to escape to the beach—without a tag team of bodyguards—whenever she needed solitude.

On the other hand, he got to live in magnificent Merrisand Castle, surrounded by art treasures that would satisfy one's need for beauty for a lifetime. And to share the lives of people like Sophie and her parents and the other children on the cruise. Annegret wouldn't have missed that experience for anything.

Who was she kidding? Fantastic as that had been, it paled beside being in Maxim's arms. The power, the pleasure were with her still, the need for a repeat compelling. The place she was in now felt like the eye of a hurricane. Turmoil behind and probably ahead. For now, stillness and a chance to catch her breath, although it was proving challenging. Maxim had done that to her.

She needed to see him. To talk about the film. Yes, that was it. To show him her progress, get his opinion on the budget. She tucked the laptop under her arm. Before she could leave the suite, the phone rang. He must want to see her, too. She snatched up the receiver, only to have joy turn to disappointment. "Oh, it's you."

"Try to contain your enthusiasm," Brett said.

"I didn't expect to hear from you."

"Obviously not, although you knew we'd have to deal with one another professionally."

Since his father owned the television network that carried her show, and Brett was head of programming, she had little choice. "I'm still on vacation for another couple of weeks," she pointed out.

"Longer than that, actually."

Feeling herself pale, she put the laptop down before she could drop it. She should have known. "So this isn't a social call?"

"You were aware of what was in the cards."

Here it comes, she thought. Pride kept the trepidation out of her voice. "Go ahead and make it official then."

"Your show won't be renewed next season. I'm sorry, Annegret."

He didn't sound sorry. She had to know. "Was it your decision or your father's?"

"Does it matter?" His voice softened. "If it helps, I argued for another chance for you. But Dad's new lady friend put her pet project in front of him and she got the nod. He's besotted with her, and overrode my objections. So this is no fault of yours. That Champagne Pact stuff you e-mailed me about sounded like a great season opener."

Not anymore. "Thank you for telling me yourself." She hadn't credited him with that much decency.

"I really am sorry," he repeated. This time she believed him.

For a long time after hanging up, she stared at the phone. Brett was right. She had known the ax could fall, but had hoped if she produced a tantalizing-enough subject, she could forestall it.

Her heart ached for all the people depending on the show. On her. She had let all of them down, including

Maxim. Slowly she got to her feet. She still wanted
to see him, but now it was to tell him she wouldn't
need the interviews, after all.

A new thought came to her. Was this how he would
feel if he forfeited his crown? Through no fault of her
own, she had failed her crew and workmates. They
would have to find other ways to pay their way, and
despite Brett's assurance, she felt wretchedly responsible. If Maxim followed his heart, he failed the hundreds of thousands of people who looked to him for
leadership.

More clearly now, she understood. But it still hurt.
As Brett's news would hurt for a long time.

Maxim was in the Round Tower, she learned when
she called his office. Any other time she would have
welcomed the excuse to go there because it was a
part of the castle she hadn't seen yet. Right now she
felt as if she would shatter into pieces if Maxim said
anything kind to her. She decided to tell him matter-
of-factly, convey her regrets and get the devil out of
there. What she really wanted to do—fall apart—
would have to wait.

She could have taken the shorter route through the
grand reception rooms and executive office complex,
across a footbridge to the elevator that had been
added discreetly to the centuries-old tower. Instead
she emerged from her suite in the royal apartments
into the sunshine and mingled with the visitors taking
tours of the castle, hoping the company would improve her mood.

It didn't. The babel of languages and the general
air of happiness hit her like an insult. Couldn't they
see that a chunk of her world had just splintered off

like a calving iceberg, leaving her adrift in a hostile sea?

She still had Maxim's project. Probably Chad's as well, if she wanted it. He was businessman enough not to reject her talents because she'd rejected him. She consoled herself by thinking she could hire some of the crew left jobless by the show's cancellation. She could live and work in Carramer for as long as she wanted. It should have cheered her. Instead, all she could think was, *without Maxim.*

That was what distressed her the most. Not losing the show, other than for the people it would hurt, but losing the chance to work so closely with him. The prospect had energized her as nothing else had ever done. No wonder working on the TV program about Maxim's family had seemed effortless, because it was *his* story. Not even planning a documentary about the Merrisand Trust would feel as satisfying.

Maxim hung up the phone, a grin almost splitting his face. Of all the calls he'd taken today, this was one for the record books. He could hardly believe what he'd just been told, but the source was impeccable, and the RPD had confirmed the caller's bona fides. Everything Maxim had been told was true. His heart felt as if it was going to burst from his chest.

His first thought was to summon Annegret and tell her everything was going to be all right between them. Their future was so bright it dazzled him.

Stopping short, he ordered himself to think. You *didn't* summon the woman you loved. Especially when she had no idea what was going on. Her world was about to be turned upside down. However hard it was, he needed to be gentle with her, give her time to deal with the changes she was about to face.

Then a servant brought the news that she was on her way, and Maxim had to think fast. He had promised the caller he wouldn't say anything to her just yet, but it was going to be difficult when he wanted to shout the news from the rooftops. He yearned to take her in his arms and kiss her until she was dizzy with wanting him, then make slow, sweet love to her from now until dawn. Knowing it was possible at last gave him the strength to wait. Delayed pleasures were the most gratifying, he told himself.

When a guard showed her in, Maxim sat behind a massive, carved ironwood table pretending to leaf through Giselle's collection of magazines. He had actually been looking at one of them when the call came. Now the pages were a blur. He could only marvel at Annegret.

Wearing a ruffled cream blouse and the pencil-slim navy skirt that made her legs look a mile long, she was a different woman from the tousled wench who'd greeted him in her cabin on the ship.

Pity, he thought, then reconsidered. It might be even more fun exploring what was beneath that chic facade.

Patience, he reminded himself.

He smiled and gestured for the guard to leave them alone. When the door closed, he said, "I was hoping you'd come."

His heated gaze mirrored her own, she knew. The two-foot-thick walls shut out the castle sounds, but not the thunder of her heartbeat. She struggled to make her tone light. "So you could show me some magazines?"

He frowned until he saw she meant the folder. "These? I was doing some research. No, I wanted you to see this room. Recognize it?"

Tearing her gaze away, she surveyed the chamber. Round, of course. Thick stone walls hung with tapestries and family portraits. Mullioned windows cleverly concealing their double glazing.

Then it came to her. "The Champagne Pact was signed here, in this room."

She prowled until she found the right angle, the one the painter had chosen to capture the moment. By accident or design, Maxim was standing in the exact spot where his ancestor had put his seal to the document. Sealing her fate, too, in a way.

The prince framed the room with his thumbs and forefingers. "For an opening scene, I thought you could start with the painting, then dissolve to this chamber, with Chad and me in the same pose as our ancestors. What do you think?"

Numb because it was perfect, she nodded. Maxim's willingness to include Chad in a scene that had to rankle touched her more deeply than he could know. Her gaze swam and she blinked hard. "It's a great idea."

Her tone betrayed her. "You aren't going to use it."

She shook her head. "My show has been cancelled." Haltingly, she explained about Brett's phone call.

Listening to her pretend she wasn't upset made Maxim see red. "That man must have rocks for brains."

She flushed and looked away. "It wasn't unexpected."

Cupping her chin between his thumb and forefinger, he made her face him. Under his thumb he felt her pulse jump. ''Repeat after me—he's a fool without an ounce of good taste.''

Her mouth trembled, but this time with faint humor. ''He's a fool without an ounce of good taste.''

''And you're much too sensitive and talented for him.''

''And I'm...oh.'' She wrenched herself free, the tremulous smile vanishing. ''Maxim, I didn't come for this.''

Because she didn't want to get involved with royalty. Now who was the fool? He had been so elated after the phone call that he had forgotten—or hadn't wanted to remember—that she didn't want any part of his life.

His vision of a shared future shattered like glass as fate's cruelty left him breathless. Finally, finally, he had found the woman of his dreams, and just moments ago he had been granted a miracle that meant they could be together. It didn't mean she would want to.

It was his own fault for avoiding reality. Annegret had made no secret of her feelings about royalty. She might change after she learned the truth about herself, but he doubted it. The attitudes of a lifetime were deeply ingrained. He saw it in the wariness in her gaze and the defensive way she held herself apart from him.

He cut off the plea that welled up. He had no right to tell her how he felt, or use the physical attraction flaming between them to force a response she might regret later. With no divorce in Carramer, she would be tied to him. If royal life proved as unpalatable to her as she expected, there would be no way out.

Giving her one now was all he could do, and it almost broke him. "I'm relieved to hear it, Annegret."

"You—you are?"

Wanting desperately to wrap his arms around her, he thrust his hands into his pockets instead. "We both feel the chemistry between us. But that's all it is. All it can be."

Her eyes glittered, making him feel brutish, but her voice was steady. "If you have something to tell me, you'd better come out with it."

"All right." He picked up the file of magazines and held it open at a cover photograph of an exotic beauty in her mid-twenties. "This is Princess Talay Rasada, the woman I'm going to marry."

Chapter Twelve

By the time Maxim finished extolling the virtues of the princess, Annegret wanted to take the first plane to Sapphan and do murder. He didn't have to tell her who Talay Rasada was. The Rasada family had provided Annegret with one of her first and most-watched programs after she'd learned that the princess had spent time in medical care in Australia as a teen-ager, following an assassination attempt on her family.

One of Talay's therapists had escorted the girl home to Sapphan. The therapist had been unaware she'd been chosen by the girl's grandfather as a suit-able match for the future king. By the time she found out, she had fallen foul of Sapphan's law stating that two people were legally married as soon as a proposal was freely made and accepted. In the therapist's case, the proposal she accepted was the king's.

That the former Norah Kelsey was still married—happily, from all accounts, and judging by their three children—and the most revered queen in Sapphan's history, didn't mitigate the circumstances, in Annegret's view. Her program had pulled no punches. The king of Sapphan had lured the woman there, deprived her of her liberty and tricked her into marriage. Now Maxim intended to marry one of that family.

She had to know. "Do you love Talay Rasada?"

His expression remained shuttered. "Love is inconsequential. As I explained, she is from a dynasty that has ruled for—"

"Seventeen centuries, I know," Annegret snapped. Would it have hurt less if he had loved the woman? To know that he didn't—and nothing in his manner suggested love—reminded her more forcibly than anything else that his world was different from hers. Royalty was different. Like the superrich in her own country, they married for alliances, for heirs, for politics.

She wasn't good enough. The whisper came from her heart and wouldn't be silenced. Just like Brett's father and her own, Maxim had rejected her because her pedigree was all wrong.

Well, not anymore. The show was over, so she was through sticking her nose in royal affairs. Investigating them had made good television, but now she saw her quest for what it was, a kind of self-deprecation impelled by her history. She was finished with that now. She would find someone else to make the Merrisand movie for Maxim, and contact Chad Soral, telling him she was, after all, available.

What she meant by that, she wasn't certain. But she was going to find out.

Not by so much as a tremor did she let her voice betray her. "I hope you'll be very happy together."

Before he could tell her that happiness was irrelevant, and explain yet again that the Champagne Pact left him no choice, she excused herself and fled back to her suite. She felt strangely calm and dry-eyed. Even a bad decision was better than none, she decided. Hers had been made. She'd meant what she'd said. She wished Maxim and his princess a good life together, and she intended to have one herself.

Refusing to let herself consider anything else, she marched into the suite and instantly sensed that someone was there. In no mood to have servants fussing around her, she stormed into the living room. "Would you kindly...um, what on earth are you doing here?"

Her mother rose gracefully and came toward Annegret with arms outstretched. "It's a welcome of sorts, although I'd prefer, 'how wonderful, I'm so glad to see you.'"

Debra was slimmer, Annegret noticed when they hugged. But it suited her, and her expression was— *glowing* was the only word she could think to use. "I *am* glad to see you. I tried to phone you this morning."

"I was on a plane by then. I came straight here to surprise you."

"You succeeded. How did you get into the castle past all the security?"

Debra's smile softened. "Your Prince Maxim made it easy for me."

Pain gripped her heart, although she pushed it away. He wasn't, never would be, *her* prince. "You've spoken to him?"

"Not directly. Someone...interceded on my behalf. Oh darling, you've no idea how much I've wanted to see you. Let me look at you."

Curbing her curiosity at the reason for her mother's unexpected arrival, Annegret allowed herself to be held at arm's length and inspected, as her mother had done since she was a little girl. "Do I pass muster?" she asked.

"I don't like the shadows around your eyes."

"Thanks, Mom, you look great, too."

Debra's lips pursed. "I'm worrying, not criticizing. Have you been working too hard?"

Annegret tugged her mother to a sofa and sat down alongside her. "A little. I've been offered two new projects since coming to Carramer."

"Darling, that's wonderful."

"It's not all good news. Brett Colton called earlier today. The network cancelled the show."

"I'm so sorry. Did Brett say why?"

Debra's gaze reflected Annegret's initial suspicion that the unhappy ending of their romance had influenced the decision. "Budget cuts are the official reason. But his father's new lady friend put up a proposal that trumped mine," she admitted.

Gripping both her hands, Debra said, "Rotten deal, but the other projects should make things easier. And I hope my news will make you feel better still."

"You're getting married."

At her stab in the dark, she actually saw her mother blush. It was such a fascinating sight that Annegret's smile broadened, and gladness for her mother welled up. "You *are*. Tell me, who's the lucky man?"

Debra hesitated, breathed deeply, then said, "Your father."

How was she supposed to react to that? "You've heard from him?" Stupid thing to say. Debra must have, if they were getting back together.

"I got in touch with him."

Questions shrilled through Annegret. Had her mother known her father's whereabouts all along? Why had she waited until now to contact him? Concern for her mother made her ask, "Are you sure it was a good idea?"

"It was…necessary. You tried to hide it, but I know you too well. I knew you were in love with Prince Maxim the moment I heard you talking about him on the phone. I had to find out if I could do anything to help."

There's nothing you can do unless you know a way to rewrite history. Her mother must have taken her at her word, and she'd done so for nothing. Since she couldn't deny the truth of Debra's conclusion, Annegret said, "You shouldn't have done that. You were better off without…" She didn't even know what to call her father.

"Frederick." Her mother filled the awkward silence. "His full name is Frederick von Taxen-Zwar."

Her breath rushed out. "Quite a mouthful. I suppose he thought it was worth renewing his interest when you told him your daughter is involved with a prince?"

Debra tensed visibly. "I'm sure you don't mean that to be as insulting as it sounds."

Shocked at herself, Annegret shook her head. "I'm sorry, it's just—it's a lot to take in." Especially coming on top of Maxim's marriage plans and the cancellation of her TV show. How much more could she absorb in one day?

"I understand. Believe me, I do. I'm still shell-shocked myself after speaking to Frederick. It's been a long time."

A lifetime. "How did you manage to contact him?"

"After hearing the news that the monarchy had been restored in Ehrenberg, I decided to call and ask for him."

"Simple as that, huh?" Pity it couldn't be so simple for her and Maxim. Annegret drove the thought away. This was about her mother's future, not hers.

"It wasn't quite as easy as I'm making it sound. During the revolutionary years, services deteriorated badly in Ehrenberg. It took me days to get through, even longer to bribe someone to connect me with Frederick."

Bribery from a woman who'd never so much as fudged her tax return? Way to go, Mom. "Have you seen him? How did you go from a phone call to making marriage plans so quickly?"

"We've been married since before you were born," her mother said, so quietly that Annegret almost missed it. "I just didn't know it."

The room seemed to reel. "You'd better start at the beginning."

"It's true that we met and fell in love while I was working at his embassy. Frederick wanted us to fly to Europe to be married in Ehrenberg, but trouble was brewing and it wasn't safe. So he arranged a quiet ceremony in Sydney. With only the minister and two strangers for witnesses, nobody thought anything of it. We planned to have a more elaborate wedding when he could safely take me back to his country, but we never got the chance. You were conceived on our wedding night."

"Why did you tell me I was born out of wedlock?"

Debra cupped her hands together as if she were

cold. "Because I believed you had been. Frederick was recalled the next day, and the revolution started within hours of his return. I was frantic with worry, but heard nothing until I got a letter from him saying he'd had our marriage annulled. He said it was for the best, and he'd deny it if I ever told anyone we'd been married."

It was Annegret's turn to feel cold. "He regretted acting in haste?"

"I thought so. By the time the letter reached me, the borders were closed and all communications cut, so I couldn't ask him to explain."

"Surely his reasoning was obvious? He'd had what he wanted from you." Like Annegret herself, her mother hadn't been good enough for a lasting relationship with a man who moved in royal circles.

Debra reached for her. "It wasn't like that. I'd have slept with him without a wedding ring if he'd asked me. He was the one who wanted us to marry."

Heartsore because Debra had believed what were obviously the man's lies, Annegret felt weary suddenly. Her opinion of her father hadn't improved. But she needed to know. "Why would you go back to a man who treated you so badly?"

"Because I never stopped loving him. None of this was his doing. When the revolution started, he and his father were arrested and sent to a former monastery in the mountains. His father died there of the hardships. To protect me, Frederick smuggled out the letter, worded so anyone who intercepted it would think our marriage was over. But it wasn't true."

Annegret felt hers eyes blur with tears. "Oh, Mom."

Debra dragged in a breath. "He said thinking of

me helped him survive. As time passed and security was relaxed, he started farming to pass the time, growing food to improve the lot of the others who'd been banished with him. He told me he lived for the time when we could be together again.''

Annegret couldn't discount the sincerity in her mother's eyes. Her father was another matter. ''Yet he waited for you to contact him?''

''I'd left the diplomatic service and moved twice, but he hadn't given up. He was still looking for me.'' The older woman's eyes glistened. ''Oh Annegret, if I hadn't called the palace on your behalf, he'd still be searching.''

''I'm happy for you, Mom, honestly, but I don't see how a minor royal functionary is supposed to help me.''

Debra rose and paced, before stopping abruptly. ''Frederick was never a minor functionary. When we met, he was crown prince of Ehrenberg. With the monarchy restored, and his father gone, he's now the king.''

Annegret's breath hissed out. At some level she'd known her mother wasn't telling her everything. ''Why did you let me think he was only a royal hanger-on?''

''For your safety. His letter was so unlike the man I knew that I was frightened. I thought if anyone learned you were his daughter, you might be in danger. So I made up the story about your father being the prince's equerry.''

''And made me into the world's most determined antiroyalist.'' She gave a shaky laugh. ''I never suspected.''

"Neither did Frederick, until he flew to Australia and I told him he had a daughter."

Tension coiled through Annegret. "How did he react?"

Debra's breath caught. "He wept with joy. He can't wait to meet you."

A lump lodged in Annegret's throat. Her father not only wanted her, but had cried at the news of her existence. The stuff of her dreams. "Does he want us to go to Ehrenberg?" she asked, feeling as emotional as her mother sounded.

"Better than that. Frederick is on his way to Carramer now. He was the one who cleared the way with Prince Maxim. I persuaded Frederick to let me come on ahead so I could talk to you first."

The break in Debra's voice told Annegret how hard the new separation had been on her mother, endured for her daughter's sake. "What was it like, seeing him again after so long?" she asked.

Debra's eyes shone. "As if we'd never been apart. This time in Carramer is going to be like the honeymoon we never finished."

Annegret clasped her mother's hands. "I'm so happy for you. Maybe I should give you two some time alone before I meet my—Frederick." When she'd dealt with the shock of having a father, let alone one who was a king.

"Frederick doesn't want to wait. He's anxious to meet you and your prince."

Thinking of how Maxim had reacted to the news that her father was King Frederick of Ehrenberg, Annegret looked away. He'd been so overcome that he'd gotten himself betrothed to a princess.

Annegret was also a princess. Maxim had known

before she did. And it hadn't made any difference. She stared down at her hands. "I'm afraid he isn't my prince, and doesn't want to be."

"I had hoped finding out about Frederick would make things easier for the two of you. I'm sorry if it hasn't."

Annegret felt her nerves jump. "There's more than a title standing between me and Maxim." Haltingly, she explained about his betrothal to Talay Rasada. "All we had was chemistry," she finished. Such chemistry, but not nearly enough.

"Are you sure? I'd hate you to waste as many years as I've done."

"You didn't have a choice. A revolution made the decision for you."

"Perhaps you need a revolution of your own, in your thinking. Maxim may be a prince, but he's first and foremost a man."

"A man who thinks an alliance between Carramer and Sapphan will be good for the economy," Annegret said tiredly, remembering Maxim's lecture. Had it only been this morning?

"He could be trying to convince himself."

"And he could believe it." She felt pain tighten her features. "He knew, Mom. He knew the Champagne Pact no longer stood in our way, and he let me walk out of there without a word. Worse, he gave me a laundry list of reasons why marrying Talay Rasada was the logical thing to do."

"I can't explain why he did that, but running away from your father won't solve anything."

Annegret gripped her elbows, hugging herself. "I'm not running away. I want to meet Frederick, just not today."

"Why not? He's a good man, Greta, and he's your father. It's bound to feel strange, but you have half his genes. You share some of his looks, and you've definitely inherited his stubbornness. Isn't it time you found out where that part of you comes from?"

It wasn't like her mother to plead. How could Annegret taint her happiness, when she'd endured so much? "All right, I'll do it for you," she conceded, feeling a flutter around the region of her heart. She suspected she wasn't agreeing only to please Debra.

She stood and her mother hugged her. "You won't regret your decision."

Annegret began to regret it as soon as she learned that Maxim would be at the airport to welcome the king. She'd assumed—hoped—that Maxim's father, as governor of the province, would officiate, but he was out of the country for a few days. And Annegret's mother had assured her daughter that King Frederick wanted to keep his visit as informal as possible.

If this was informal, she didn't want to be part of a state occasion, Annegret thought as she looked around next morning. There was no red carpet or brass band, but the flag of Ehrenberg flew alongside the Carramer flag atop the main airport concourse. A small contingent of solders stood guard near the private airstrip where the king's plane was expected to land.

Their spit and polish made Annegret uneasy. She had spent the night tossing and turning, trying to deal with the news that she was a princess by birth. After making a career of exposing the foibles of the world's royalty, she found it a shock to learn she was one of them.

•

Not that she intended to let it change anything. She had reluctantly agreed to her mother's wish that she return with them to Ehrenberg, but had vetoed any suggestion that she take up royal life.

"I'll leave that to you," she'd told her mother fondly. "After the experience you got wrestling the boardinghouse into shape, getting a whole country back on its feet should be a piece of cake."

Debra was looking forward to it, she knew. Beneath the bridal nerves, which were perfectly understandable, her mother couldn't wait to get her teeth into this new challenge. With the love of her life at her side, she could do anything, she'd told Annegret.

A surge of jealousy made Annegret sway. Why couldn't it be so simple for her? But Maxim's attitude toward her hadn't changed. As they assembled to welcome the king's plane, he addressed her as "Your Highness" and she told him abruptly to cut it out.

"I'm no more a princess than I was yesterday."

He gave her a strange look, almost as if she'd disappointed him in some way. Surely it should have been the other way around? "I see that discovering your birthright hasn't mellowed your attitude."

She let her silence speak for her. He was the one marrying Princess Talay for economic reasons. Annegret had thought, had truly believed, that he cared about her and only the Champagne Pact was standing in their way.

Now, an arm's length away from him, she knew better. Maxim might want her in his bed—his kisses leaving her in no doubt—but that was all. How much she wanted to *be* in his bed she was mortified to think. She still wanted him, pity help her. Wanted to feel his arms around her and his mouth claiming hers so badly that she ached.

Betrayal, anger, hurt. None of them could touch the overwhelming sense of rightness she'd felt in his arms. Would never feel again.

"All I have is a title," she told him, holding herself stiffly against the desire to reach out. "It doesn't change anything." Obviously not Maxim's plan to marry someone else.

He remained stony, eyes to the front. "If that's how you want it, I respect your decision."

Respect was so far from what she needed from him that she nearly said so. Heat raged through her, made up of equal parts temper and desire. Why didn't he argue, rant, rave, throw her over his shoulder and carry her off to his castle? He wouldn't because he was a prince and had other priorities, she reminded herself.

Two could play this game. She might not have much experience of being a princess, but she could act as cool and aloof as Maxim. As if her heart wasn't breaking, she readied herself to meet her father for the first time in her life.

Chapter Thirteen

It was a different Annegret who stood on the Merrisand wharf a few months later, her field of vision filled by the great white cruise ship. She and her film crew had finished work for the day. They were packing up around her, giving her time to look at the *Princess of the Isles* riding serenely at anchor, and remember.

Later today the ship would cast off on another voyage on behalf of the Merrisand Trust. Was it really only a couple of months since she'd been aboard the inaugural cruise as Maxim's guest, planning to make a film about the trust?

Although she'd been back in Merrisand for almost five weeks, she still hadn't done anything about that, and the prince hadn't asked, although he knew she was now working for Chad Soral because Chad had told her of meeting the prince. Maxim had sent his regards.

His regards.

As an engaged man he couldn't very well send anything else, she told herself. But his coldness still hurt.

Telling herself it was familiar territory, not because she wanted to be close to the prince, she'd rented a house in Merrisand after spending time in Ehrenberg with her parents.

Her father—how strange it felt, although she was getting used to it—had told her she was welcome to stay if she wanted to. But the ancient stone buildings and misty mountains hadn't felt like home. She was a child of the southern hemisphere, of mild, wet winters and melting summers, of beaches and rain forests and colors vibrant enough to dazzle the eyes. Although she was touched by the way the people of Ehrenberg took her and her mother to their hearts, she couldn't imagine settling there permanently.

Knowing her mother was happy was enough for Annegret. King Frederick was a good man with a gentle, almost scholarly manner. She'd been surprised by how much she liked her father. After his years out of power, he described himself as more farmer than monarch. He hadn't expected her to accept him instantly, but had given her the time and space she needed to come to terms with her new existence. If she'd had her pick of fathers, she couldn't have done better, she decided.

When she'd told him so, his eyes had misted, she remembered fondly. "You're a daughter any man would be proud to claim," he'd assured her. "From what your mother said, I was afraid you'd hate the life of a princess."

She would have guaranteed it, until she tried it. The camaraderie she'd found among the people of Ehrenberg, who had little enough of anything else, brought out a selflessness she hadn't known she possessed.

Letting herself be acclaimed as their princess, even making an effort to look the part, was little enough to do to help her father's people. She masked her discomfort at being curtsied to and fussed over, telling herself that the people of Ehrenberg needed the visible signs that their monarch was back to stay. She even started to enjoy herself.

"It kills me to have my every whim catered to, but somebody has to do it," she'd told the king with a theatrical sigh.

His gentle smile had widened. "You think I haven't seen how hard you and your mother have been working? You are allowed to refuse some engagements."

Her shoulders had lifted. "How do I choose who needs me the most?"

A long silence had followed before he said, "You really are my daughter."

Recalling the note of pride in his voice, she was glad she'd stayed. Glad she'd made herself useful. More comfortable being behind a camera than in front of one, she'd even agreed to be interviewed so the international media could highlight the country's need. As a result, aid was pouring in.

Much remained to be done to bring Ehrenberg back to its former glory, but that was work for other hands. She'd done what she could. With her parents' blessing, she'd slipped quietly out of the country.

Maxim wasn't the reason she had returned to Carramer, she told herself fiercely. With no job for her in Australia, she'd taken up Chad's offer to document the work of the Soral Shipping Line on film. A few

of her old crew had followed her to Carramer, and
she'd found a supply of promising interns at the film
academy. They wanted her to teach there, too. She
was considering it.

'Hey, princess, is that it for the day?''

Lost in thought, she hadn't heard Chris, her Australian location manager, approach. His reference to
the title she hadn't used since coming back to Carramer was a standing joke between them. "Yes, we're
done here. Tell you what—you've done such a great
job, why don't you take the next three days off?''

He rolled his eyes. "You're all heart, considering
it's the Journey Day weekend and we get Monday
off, anyway.''

Her playful push sent him on his way. "Don't say
I never do you any favors.''

Journey Day was the Carramer holiday commem-
orating the journey of the prince who'd traveled
around the islands, uniting them into one kingdom.
The historic journey was reenacted in schools
throughout the country, and children received gifts,
usually toy boats, to wish them well on their life's
journey.

"You want to join us for coffee?'' Chris asked.

She shook her head. "You go ahead. I'll be fine.''

Where was her life's journey taking her? she wondered, watching her crew drive off. She didn't regret
not joining them. She planned to hang around for a
while. Maybe she'd run into some of the families
from the first cruise. She'd heard from Sophie's parents that the child had been in remission long enough
to be considered cured, so she wasn't likely to be
aboard, praise be. But there were others Annegret was
still concerned about.

Odd that the wharf wasn't bustling with activity. Chad could have mistaken the time of sailing. Today they'd only planned to film some background footage, so the sailing time wasn't important, but it seemed strange to see only the crew going about their tasks. Their lack of urgency suggested nothing was going to happen for some hours.

Curious now, she decided to step aboard and find out what was going on.

Walking up the gangway and onto the deck gave her a not-unpleasant sense of déjà vu. Warmth washed over her. It was here that Maxim had taken her in his arms on a moonlit night, here that she had discovered she loved him. She'd thought she was over all that, but the sights, sounds and scents of the ship brought back the feelings so strongly that she gripped the white railing for support.

"I hoped you would come."

The sound of Maxim's voice was so real that she closed her eyes. On this morning's news there'd been an announcement that Princess Talay of Sapphan would be visiting Carramer in the summer. Knowing the reason, Annegret had been swept by a sense of desolation. It must be why she imagined hearing Maxim's voice now.

"I was almost ready to carry you aboard myself."

"No." The desolate, keening sound couldn't possibly have come from her. She needed to get a grip fast.

Then he took her in his arms and she knew he was real. When he pulled her into the shadow of a bulkhead and crushed his mouth against hers, she couldn't help it. She answered him out of her own desperate need, opening to him and feeling her heart thunder against his chest.

For an age, she could only take and take, feeling her heart squeeze dry of everything but desire. All the time she'd been away she had longed for this. For him.

Sanity seeped back much too slowly. Wild-eyed, she struggled to free herself even as he held her tightly. "Let me go," she insisted, and wasn't especially happy when he complied. "I can't do this anymore. It's too hard."

"You came back," he said.

"For myself. Not for you."

"Are you quite sure?"

She tossed her head. In Europe her hair had grown longer, making the gesture more satisfying. "You flatter yourself. I came back because I love Carramer. I have work here. Let me go."

He tugged on her hand, spinning her back into his arms, ignoring her attempt to free herself. "Stop fighting me. I'm trying to talk you."

She made herself stay still, although her pulse was racing. "This isn't talking." Aware that her resistance was dangerously low, she added, "The passengers will be arriving soon. I have to go."

"Go where?"

He turned her so she could see the yawning gap of water between ship and shore. Focused on him, she hadn't noticed them start to move. "What do you think you're doing?"

"Taking you out to sea. Only a little way. We'll be back in time for the passengers to come aboard."

No wonder there were no other passengers in sight. "Did you mislead Chad about the time of sailing, to lure me here early?'' she demanded, infusing her tone with annoyance at his high-handedness.

''I didn't have to. It was his idea.''

Her head began to spin. ''That's crazy. Turn the ship around now.''

''Not until we have a chance to talk.''

Pain like fire burned through her. In a heartbeat he had made nonsense of her delusion that she was over him. She would never be over him. But she would survive. ''I'm not interested, so you may as well tell the crew to take me back to the wharf.''

She was talking to herself. Clutching her hand, he towed her forward to a covered deck where a huge woven hammock swayed with the ship. The ropes holding the hammock were garlanded with flowers, and blossoms were twined around every stanchion on the deck.

Perfumes scented the air—rose, jasmine, ginger. There was even a Janus lily in full bloom. A shiver of memory rippled through her, although the flower had been carefully placed where it could be admired but not touched.

It was a setting for seduction.

She was aware of Maxim watching for her reaction. ''I've given orders that no one is to come near this deck,'' he said when she stayed silent.

At the sight of so much beauty, an avalanche of emotions clamored for release. She couldn't allow it. ''Aren't you forgetting something? Your fiancée?''

His gaze darkened. ''My what?''

''Princess Talay Rasada.'' The words hurt Anne-gret's throat, but she made herself say them, for herself as much as for him.

''Talay isn't my fiancée.''

"Perhaps not yet."

He gripped her arms. "Not ever. How can I marry her or anyone, when I'm—"

Annegret pressed her fingers to his mouth. "Her visit was announced on the news this morning."

He lifted her hand away, but didn't release it. "To study the work of the Merrisand Trust so she can set up a similar organization in Sapphan. My father hoped something would happen between us, but it's too late."

Determined not to cry, Annegret snapped at him instead. "That's the first true thing you've said. It's too late."

"I don't believe it, and I don't think you do, either."

"You don't want to believe it. You're so used to getting your own way."

His mouth twisted wryly. "I doubt that will be the case after we're married."

"We're not getting married." Anger swirled through her and she clung to it, fighting the floral perfume fogging her senses. "You knew I was a princess before I did, yet you said nothing."

"King Frederick asked me to let your mother break the news to you. It was killing me not to let you know that there were no more impediments between us."

"You showed me Talay's picture and said you were going to marry her. That doesn't sound like a man who wants us to be together. Unless—" affront threaded her tone "—I won't be your mistress."

Maxim didn't look as shocked as she thought he should. "Chad bet me you'd say that."

She drew herself up. "So I've become a joke between you? I thought he was your rival."

The prince looked rueful. "So did I. Until I learned that he courted you to make me jealous enough to do precisely what I'm doing now."

She still didn't understand, and wasn't sure she wanted to. "Whatever's going on between you has nothing to do with me."

"It has everything to do with you. When we were younger Chad took advantage of his position to steal a woman I cared about. Evidently he's regretted his actions for a long time. When he saw how I felt about you, he decided to make amends."

"By using me? I don't think—"

Maxim didn't let her finish. "Sit down. Please."

The hammock offered the only place to sit. She sat on the edge, stilling its movement by planting her feet on the deck. The sooner she let him talk, the quicker this would be over. "Very well, I'm listening."

The prince steadied himself by holding one of the flower-bedecked ropes. "At first, when I discovered you were a princess by birth, I was overjoyed. Not even the Champagne Pact could keep us apart any longer."

The flowers crushed under his hand enveloped her in the fragrance of jasmine. She felt herself falling, and tightened her hold on the edge of the hammock. "Then why pretend you were marrying Talay?"

"You reminded me how much you dislike royal life. Knowing that, how could I tie you to it for a lifetime? I love you too much. Breaking my own heart was a small price to pay to keep yours whole."

Caught up in her own pain, she hadn't considered his. Could he really have been trying to protect her? She saw the truth shimmering in his gaze as he looked at her. "Oh, Maxim, I never suspected." A moment later, "I had a lot to learn," she admitted.

"You learned it well. The woman I saw on television, speaking for the people of Ehrenberg, looked every inch a princess. I saw how you offered comfort, encouragement and hope. Not once did you look as if it was a hardship for you. In fact you seemed to be enjoying yourself. That's when I dared to think—no hope—there could be a chance for us."

Her own hope was almost painful. "I didn't think about being a princess. All I cared about was making a difference."

"You made it. You can do it again, here in Carramer. Being royal opens doors, makes it possible to perform miracles."

She nodded. "As I learned in Ehrenberg."

"Come back to me, Annegret. Rule at my side. Letting you walk away from me almost tore out my heart. I don't think I can survive it a second time."

Again she felt the strong pull of desire. The sting of happy tears. "I want to."

"I'll never hurt you again, I promise. I want us to be together for always. Marry me and we'll fill Merrisand Castle with children who'll never have to choose between their heritage and their heart's desires, as we almost had to do. That is, if you love me as much as I love you."

She looked up at him, seeing him sway slightly with the movement of the ship, or the force of his emotions. Her prince. Her beloved. He had been willing to give her up rather than condemn her to a life he thought would make her unhappy.

There was only one answer she could give. "Yes.

There aren't words enough to express how much I love you.''

"Carramer has the words.'' Coming to sit beside her, he tipped her back into the hammock until she lay in his arms. Stroking her face tenderly, he murmured what she recognized were the most intimate of his native language's many expressions of love.

She had no need to know the foreign-sounding words to understand his meaning, because she felt it in his embrace. The same message was in her own eyes as she looked at him. "I will love you forever and always.''

Epilogue

When Annegret told Maxim how much she loved flowers, she had never expected he would fill the grand reception room of Merrisand Castle with them, thousands upon thousands of tropical blooms that competed with the gardens outside for sheer beauty.

He wanted their wedding day to be perfect, she knew. Didn't he know that as long as he waited for her at the altar, it couldn't be anything else?

Readying herself for the walk down the endless red carpet to his side, she stopped to peer around the vestibule door. Maxim was talking softly to his groomsmen, Eduard, Marquis of Merrisand, his brother-in-law, Bryce Laws, and their cousin, Rowe Sevrin, Viscount Aragon. They made an impressive group. But she had eyes only for Maxim, looking impossibly handsome in full morning dress.

Her father saw her peeking. "Bet the groom looks as nervous as you feel," he whispered in her ear as they waited for the bridal march to start.

She shot King Frederick a worried look. "Does it show?"

"Not outwardly, so relax. You look absolutely beautiful." He tucked her hand into the crook of his arm. "I'm the only one who can feel you trembling."

"With happiness," she assured him. And anticipation at the joyous future about to unfold before her. "All right, maybe I am a little nervous."

"Who wouldn't be, with half the world's crowned heads gathered under one roof? Just remember you belong here as much as any of them."

"I know."

She was no longer overwhelmed at finding herself in the company of people like Prince Lorne, the ruler of Carramer. Very soon now they would be cousins by marriage. As would his wife, Princess Alison. When Annegret had looked out into the great hall she'd seen them with their children, taking their places at the front. Seated near the monarch was Lorne's brother, Michel, and sister, Adrienne, and their families, along with the crown regent of Valmont Province, Josquin, his wife, Sarina, and their son, Christophe.

Chad Soral was there, too, looking insufferably pleased with himself. Beside him was the blond woman Annegret recognized from the first cruise.

The rest of the family and guests blurred, and Annegret blinked as she moved back from the door. It was enough to feel the love and support emanating in waves from the assembled guests.

Maxim's parents, Gabriel and Marie de Marigny, had arrived at the castle a few days before. When Maxim had taken her to Taures to meet them, Annegret had warmed to Prince Gabriel immediately, seeing how distinguished Maxim was going to look at the same age. Princess Marie was so terrifyingly regal that Annegret still felt edgy around her future mother-in-law. But she had seen enough of Marie's sense of humor under her very proper demeanor that she looked forward to them becoming friends.

Behind Annegret there was much whispering as the bridal party sorted itself out. Princess Giselle and Annegret's friend Donna were matrons of honor, while Bryce and Giselle's daughter, Amanda, and two of Annegret's Australian film crew were her bridesmaids.

The first notes of the prelude sounded. It was time. Footmen in dress uniform swung open the heavy doors. Prince Lorne's little boy, Nori, and Viscount Aragon's son, Jeffrey, began conscientiously strewing flower petals along the red carpet. If some of them were aimed at each other...well, little boys would be little boys.

"Don't you think the rose petals are overkill?" Annegret murmured.

Her father smiled. "When you and Debra planned this, I don't think you expected Maxim to raid every flower garden in Carramer. Seeing how far he's willing to go for you, I think the prince is in big trouble."

Indignation made Annegret draw herself up. "Thanks a lot."

"I mean it in the nicest possible way. He's as besotted with you as I am with your mother."

Her mother—how strange it still was to think of her as Queen Debra of Ehrenberg—was surrounded by her retinue and surreptitiously wiping away a tear.

"If Maxim and I are half as happy as you are now, I can't ask for more," Annegret affirmed.

At the altar Maxim anxiously shifted from one foot to the other. "What's taking her so long?" he asked his groomsmen in lowered tones.

Eduard grinned. "The bride's father is probably trying to talk her out of making the biggest mistake of her life."

Maxim felt himself blanch. "You don't think she's changed her mind?"

"Probably several times by now," Rowe contributed cheerfully. "The day I married Kirsten, she told me she almost turned tail and ran. And that lady doesn't run from anything."

"Kirsten has a better instinct for self-preservation than you realize," Eduard chimed in. Maxim had to remind himself that it wasn't good form to punch his cousin, especially when he was only trying to make him feel better.

Bryce patted his shoulder. "Every man goes through this on the big day, Max. But things usually turn out fine. After that, the first ten years of marriage are the hardest."

Make that two groomsmen he would have to flatten, Maxim thought. He was debating how he could make it look like an accident when Eduard nudged him. "Remember, you have the Merrisand legend on your side. It guarantees that anyone who serves the trust is rewarded by finding true love."

The other man nodded and Rowe said, "Listen to the marquis, Max. The legend worked for him, and for Giselle. As well as for Kirsten and me."

At the timely reminder, Maxim felt his apprehension ease. The legend *was* on his side. As administrator, he had thought he had been serving the trust all along. But he hadn't really understood the concept of service until he was willing to give up Annegret for her own sake. That sacrifice had shown him that true service involved the heart, not just the intellect. Evidently some lessons could only be learned the hard way.

Eduard jogged his elbow. "Here they come now."

The first triumphal notes of music soared to the hall's vaulted ceiling and he saw Annegret start down the aisle, gripping her father's arm tightly. Maxim felt his heart seize. Dressed in a trailing white gown covered in seed pearls, with a froth of chiffon around her bare shoulders, she looked like an angel.

His angel.

Her face was veiled and he knew a moment of panic as she reached beneath the wispy material to dab at her eyes. As she drew near he had to stop himself from ruining everything by sweeping her into his arms and kissing her tears away.

Time enough to do that later, when they weren't surrounded by most of Carramer's royal family and a daunting number of cameras transmitting the ceremony throughout the kingdom.

He looked down as rose petals rained on his shoes, then saw the two pages being hustled to their places by their respective mothers. Then he had eyes for no one else but his bride.

Beneath her veil, Annegret dabbed furtively at her eyes. She was not going to cry. Not when she was happier than she had ever been in her life. Everyone she cared about was here, including the man she was going to spend the rest of her life loving.

Was it really less than a year since she'd attended the wedding of her friend Donna to castle security man Kevin Jordan, in this very hall?

Earlier, as their attendants had helped them to dress, Donna had told Annegret she'd been thinking the same thing. "Imagine if I hadn't invited you to my wedding, or if you'd been unable to come all the way from Australia," she'd murmured.

Annegret knew it couldn't have happened. "Some things are meant to be." After the trials her parents had endured before being reunited, Annegret believed it with all her heart.

Marriage was working out well for Donna and Kevin, too. Annegret smiled, thinking of how her friend's bridesmaid dress had had to be altered a few days ago because she was expecting a baby. Annegret's first godchild. How long would it be before she and Maxim needed godparents for their own children?

The music swelled. "Ready?" King Frederick asked.

Annegret nodded. Without knowing it, she'd been ready for this day for most of her life. Feeling her nerves steady and her tears vanish, she moved forward, her gaze fixed on the man she loved.

"From this day forward…"

"Forsaking all others…"

"For richer, for poorer…"

"Until death do you part."

"I do."

Throughout the island kingdom, in cities and

towns, rain forests and reefs, there was universal agreement. The handsome couple couldn't be more perfectly matched. And all of Carramer rejoiced with their prince and his bride.

* * * * *

The adventure continues!
The next Carramer story will be
Operation: Monarch!
But this time look for Valerie's story in
Silhouette Intimate Moments
in January 2004 (#1268)!

COMING NEXT MONTH

#1702 RULES OF ENGAGEMENT—Carla Cassidy
Marrying the Boss's Daughter
Nate Leeman worked best alone, yet Wintersoft's senior VP
now found himself the reluctant business partner to computer
guru—and ex-girlfriend—Kat Sanderson. The hunky executive
knew business and pleasure didn't mix. So why was he suddenly looking forward to long hours and late nights with his capti-
vating co-worker?

#1703 THE BACHELOR BOSS—Julianna Morris
Sweet virgin Libby Dumont's former flame was now her
boss? She'd shared one far-too-intimate kiss with the confirmed
bachelor a decade ago, and although Neil O'Rourke was as
handsome as ever, she knew he must remain off-limits. She
just had to focus on business—*not* Neil's knee-weakening kisses!

#1704 BABY, OH BABY!—Teresa Southwick
If Wishes Were…
When Rachel Manning spoke her secret wish—to have a
baby—she never expected to become an instant mother. She
didn't even have a boyfriend! Yet here she was, temporary parent for a sweet month-old infant. Until Jake Fletcher—
the baby's take-charge, heartbreaker-in-a-Stetson-and-jeans
uncle—showed up and suggested sharing more than late-night
feedings….

#1705 THE BABY CHRONICLES—Lissa Manley
Aiden Forbes was in trouble! He hadn't seen Colleen Stewart
since she walked out on him eight years ago. Now he had
been teamed with the marriage-shy journalist to photograph
an article on babies, and seeing Colleen surrounded by all
these adorable infants was giving Aiden ideas about a baby
of their own!

SRCNM1203